# Death in Ravenna

# Richard Blake

Copyright © Richard Blake 2015

The right of Richard Blake to be identified as the author of this work has been asserted by him in accordance with the Copyright, Designs and Patents Act, 1988.

First published in 2015 by Endeavour Press Ltd.
This edition published in 2016 by Endeavour Press

## Historical Introduction

If I were writing a novel about the murder of Julius Caesar, or Nero's persecution of the Church, my duty would still be to give my absolute best. The reading public deserves no less, and it contains harsher critics than worked for any newspaper. Even so, writing in these periods would allow me to leave significant parts of the background to the reader's own historical awareness. There have been so many plays and films and novels and television productions, not to mention popular histories, that the wider issues of place and chronology could be taken for granted.

But I am writing a novel set in the seventh century – *after* the Roman Empire is often believed to have fallen. We have a continuing Empire, but with a new capital, and altered frontiers, and a solidly-established Christian Faith, and much else that may surprise the habitual reader of novels set in the Early Empire.

I know when I am being patronised, and I resent it. I do not want to patronise, or to be resented. People are increasingly aware that the Roman Empire did not fall in 476 AD. I work hard in my Byzantine novels to integrate background into the plot. At the same time, I do appreciate that some readers would like some kind of historical background to a novel set in an unfamiliar period. If you are not one of these readers, please feel free to ignore next few pages – though I still commend the map given at the end of this novel. Otherwise, here is my attempt at a potted history of the Later Roman Empire.

In 395 AD, following a century of experiment, the Roman Empire was divided into Eastern and Western administrative zones, with joint Emperors in Rome and in Constantinople. The purpose was to let each Emperor deal with the pressure on his own critical frontiers – the barbarians along the Rhine and Danube frontiers in the West, and the Persians along the Euphrates and desert frontiers in the East.

In theory, each Emperor was equal. In practice, the Eastern Emperor, ruling from Constantinople, was soon the senior partner. During the next two hundred years, becoming increasingly Greek in language in culture, the Eastern Empire flourished, and Constantinople became one of the largest and most opulent cities in the world.

The Western Empire went into immediate and rapid decline. In 406 AD, barbarians crossed the Rhine in large numbers, and broke into Italy. In 410 AD, they sacked Rome. By then, the Western Capital had been moved to Ravenna, a city in North Eastern Italy, impregnable behind marshes, and within easier reach of the frontiers – and within easy reach of Constantinople.

During the next seventy years, the Barbarians took France and Spain and North Africa from the Empire. Britain remained in the Empire, but its people were told to look to their own defence. In 476 AD, the last Western Emperor was deposed. By 500 AD, the whole of the Western Empire had been replaced by a patchwork of barbarian kingdoms.

After 527 AD, the Emperor Justinian began to reach out from Constantinople to reconquer the lost Western provinces. He recovered North Africa and Italy and part of Spain. However, the effort was exhausting. After his death in 568, the Empire lost much of Italy to the Lombard barbarians, and Rome itself fell under papal domination. Slavic and Avar barbarians crossed the Danube and conquered and burned all the way to Athens and the walls of Constantinople. After 602, the Persians began a war of destruction against the Empire. Though they ultimately lost, they did briefly take Egypt and Syria.

This novel opens in September 618 AD, and its action takes place in Ravenna and in Pavia, both cities in Northern Italy. As said, Justinian reconquered Italy in the middle of the sixth century, but much of it was lost, after 568 AD, to the Lombards. These were a new and at first a most savage race of barbarians. They were also highly intelligent. Within a generation, they had converted to Christianity, and their higher classes had adopted both Latin and the wider Roman culture. Their ambition was to become the rulers of a Latin and Christian and prosperous Italy, more or less at peace with the Eastern Empire. Their capital was Pavia. Governed by an Exarch, or Imperial Viceroy, the remaining Imperial possessions in Italy had their capital in Ravenna.

I turn to the characters. The protagonist, Roderic of Aquileia – usually known as Rodi – is a young barbarian who made his first appearance in my earlier novel, *Game of Empires*. He is an agent in the Imperial secret service, and is in Ravenna on a spying mission. It goes without saying that he did not exist. Nor did his colleagues, Cosmas, an Egyptian monk, and Synesius, a sinister old man of dubious origin and motives. Nor did Alaric, Rodi's ultimate superior, who makes no appearance in this novel, but who is the narrator of six other of my Byzantine novels.

Though he may seem one of the more unlikely characters, the Exarch Eleutherius, *did* exist. I will say no more about him here, as he will be one of the main characters in the next novel in the series, and I want to keep some element of surprise for the reader.

Of the Lombard characters, only Aripert did not exist – though someone like him surely did. I made him up on the spur of the moment, and like him a lot. He would have graced any of the Medici or Borgia courts. He will be one of the dominating characters in the sequel. If I can keep him alive, he may dominate several more.

King Adalward existed. So did General Sundarit. So did the King's mother.

Because they are so barbarous and alien, I have, in general, limited my use of Lombard names. Aripert is rather easy. But Adalward I mention only once, and I use the least unpronounceable spelling I could find. I have to mention Sundarit many times. Again, though, I use a manageable spelling. I never mention the name of the King's mother. Though not impossible to pronounce or remember, why inflict *Theudelinda* on my readers if it can be avoided?

For the seven other novels by Richard Blake set in this period, see the note at the end of this novel.

## Part One – Ravenna, Wednesday the 20th September, 618 AD

# I

Eunuchs can't grow beards. Everyone knows that. No balls, no beard. An Exarch, on the other hand – an Exarch of *Ravenna*, no less – why, everyone knows he needs a beard. He represents the Emperor. For all the power he wields, and this far from Constantinople, he might as well *be* the Emperor. He *must* have a beard. No beard, no Exarch. Everyone knows that. So when the Exarch happens to be a eunuch, there's both a problem and an obvious solution.

But it was a hot afternoon, going on evening. Eleutherius had got up to speak with his false beard tied in just the right place. Now it was slipping. Though it felt an age, he hadn't been speaking that long. It was sweat that had loosened the straps. In time to the movement of his jaw, the braided green silk was bobbing up and down half an inch below jowly flesh. Dinner must be spoiled. Some of the old men in the room were swaying from tiredness and the heat. All the same, there was the Emperor's birthday to be marked, and it was Eleutherius who was marking it. Two good reasons for not daring to sit down – nor for escaping the invisible fog of stale sweat and stinking breath that filled the big dining room.

This last didn't apply to Rodi. So long as he's not cutting purses, no one cares what a boy does. Unless he's prettier than Rodi had so far turned out, no one looks at him. He'd made sure to be at the back of the audience. Beside him, sweltering in his abbot's robe, Cosmas had propped himself against one of the columns and fallen asleep. Rodi had known he'd finally do that. He'd not miss the whispered translation from droned, soporific Latin into Greek. No one else would miss Rodi.

Slowly, a half step at a time, he backed away. He was behind another of the columns. He could still hear Eleutherius, but was out of sight. He looked round. The door for the serving slaves was open and unattended. Through the door was a small room, where the courses would eventually be stacked for serving. From there a staircase led to the kitchens on the ground floor of the fortified Residency. The staircase didn't matter. What did matter was the serving room's window. A quick casing the day before had shown that it looked into just the right place in the central courtyard.

Eleutherius was approaching first refill of the water clock. If the text wheedled out of Antony was being followed exactly, the speech had miles yet to go. The Exarch had reached the Emperor's coronation after the *coup* against wicked old Phocas. After another long sentence, he'd get to the ponderous joke about the pigeons in the Imperial Palace. At the pace he was going, he'd get to another refill of the clock, and half that again, before he sat down to call for the first course of wine.

Rodi peered around the column for a final check that all was in order. His heart skipped a beat. Where was Antony? He'd not seen or heard the Exarch's secretary leave through the big doors. But it was one of the doddery eunuchs now holding up the sheets of papyrus for the Exarch to read. *Where was Antony? When and why had he left his post?* The whole staff was supposed to be in here. If Antony was missing, the risk was too great. Rodi would have to abort the mission. There would be another opportunity.

But the serving door was open. Two weeks he and Cosmas had been in Ravenna. His instructions were to get the dirt and make straight for Constantinople. If there was another opportunity, how long before it could be this good? Antony had mentioned a "delivery" the night before last. Except for Antony not being currently where he should be – and he might not have left the room – everything was lined up for as smooth a mission as Rodi had planned. Far off in Constantinople, the Lord Treasurer Alaric would clap him on the back for the report he'd eventually make.

Cosmas hadn't moved. No one else would miss Rodi. No one else seemed to have noticed him. He was only a boy, and not a pretty one. He made up his mind. A full step, and he was inside the serving room.

## II

Until the slaves were called up by a bell cord beside the Exarch, the room would be empty. Rodi hurried to the window and looked out. No one below. The bronze downpipe was a yard to his left. He looked up. It would be a bigger jump to the sill than he fancied. But he'd known worse.

He stepped back and pulled off and folded his outer robe. He kicked off shoes that must be too big for anyone of fifteen, and that Rodi could only wear by packing them out with strips of linen. He put shoes and robe out of sight behind a cupboard. In shirt and leggings the colour of stonework, he climbed onto the sill and reached for the pipe. None of its fixings seemed to be loose. This sort of thing was always a risk. Unlike Antony, though, it was a risk he could calculate. Thoughts of the missing secretary took him back to the speech. He sat on the sill and listened. Eleutherius was ploughing through the quote from the Emperor's coronation promise. Time enough for the job in hand. He'd have to make sure it was enough.

Rodi put on gloves of leather soaked in urine till it was soft as the skin of his hands, and far less likely to slip on the age-weathered bronze. He stood up again. This time, his mind a careful blank, he leaned over and took the pipe in both hands.

It was a slow climb to the upper window. It took three scary swings into nothing before his foot made contact with the sill. From here, it was an easy jump to the floor of the Exarch's private office.

All was going as planned. The room was empty, its door locked. No sound from the smaller office beyond the door. The only sound in here was that of a late summer fly. Rodi looked about. Where to start? As you'd expect, the Exarch's office was a vast space, lush with marble and hanging silk. But Eleutherius wasn't a man who let his business pile up. Whether sitting through another batch of treason trials or dealing with reports on the water supply, the Exarch was always brisk. His desk was clear. A glance at the filing racks showed everything in place and neatly labelled. What Rodi was looking for wouldn't have been left in plain view.

He opened the nearest of the two cupboards flanking an icon of the Emperor. On every shelf, stacks of unused papyrus. Like rain through opened shutters, its bright, aromatic smell poured all about him. Nothing here. The next cupboard was locked. One poke with his thin metal probe was enough to show the lock had steel tumblers. A good place to start his search.

Given the right determination, there isn't a lock that can't be picked, and Rodi was determined. But it was a matter of the time. He looked out of the window. The sun was long out of sight behind the Residency's western wing. The sky was turning red. Three floors down, Eleutherius must be glossing over the disastrous loss of Syria and Egypt to the Persians. From this, he'd pass to the Emperor's greater success in sorting out the Church. Rodi had time for the job. But there was none to be wasted. He closed his eyes and felt about for the lock's internal geometry.

With a soft click, the tumblers gave way to the second assault. The cupboard door swung noiselessly open. Rodi stood away to see and memorise the position of all the objects. No need for the moment to go through the neatly-stacked documents. They all looked official, and therefore useless. But the lower part of the cupboard was taken up by an ebony chest. This also had a steel lock. He looked again out of the window. Assuming he was running the Exarch's speech in his head at the right speed, there was still time. More careful probing to get the chest open.

The topmost of the leather bags heaped in the chest was untied. Not moving it, Rodi could see it was filled with gold coins. An Exarch always has need of walking-about cash. But there must have been a few hundred pounds weight of the stuff here. Why not keep this much in the Treasury?

The answer lay in the papyrus sheet on top of the bags. Written backwards in what must be the Exarch's own left hand, it recorded every payment over the previous eighteen months. It all tallied with the dates – the pirate raid on Corfu, the loss of the copper fleet, the ransom given for the Bishop of Ragusa, the sale into slavery of the captives from Bari. Even in his crimes, Eleutherius was a man of careful business.

He sat on the floor to read the next sheet. It was in the same left-handed script, but was more damning still. Word had got back to Constantinople that Eleutherius was on the take from the Adriatic pirates. Here was evidence that he was directing them.

Rodi blinked and read a second time, and a third. What he'd expected to find was hard to say. But it involved hints and partial evidences of guilt that would need to be pieced together. This was like winning a whole game of dice with one roll. *He'd got the Exarch*. Recalled for questioning, Eleutherius could have a go at denying his guilt. Tried before the Emperor, he'd probably get off. Eunuchs have no friends but each other. The Imperial Palace was thick with them, and they always looked after their own. Then again, he wasn't the sort who'd take that sort of chance. He'd go in private before Alaric and strike a deal. For what he'd done, the least he deserved was to spend the rest of his life grinding corn by hand. The most Alaric would give him was a crushing fine and retirement to what was left of his estates.

None of this was Rodi's concern. Nor would he complain if the Exarch had been a fool in his making and keeping of records. Rodi's job was to get the dirt and get out. A fortnight before, he'd arrived by road, with a monk and an old man for company. No one could associate him with the fast ship apparently laid up in the harbour. Even the captain wouldn't know his instructions till the password was given. Cosmas would take a little pushing. But he could have all three of them out at sea long before Eleutherius came up to run the gold through his fingers, or whatever it was eunuchs did when no one was watching.

There was something more in the chest. It was half-under one of the bags, and had been entirely covered by the papyrus. Noting its position, he pulled it free – a parchment sheet, folded over and over again, and sealed and resealed with wax. There was nothing written on the outside. More incriminating evidence by the look of it.

He'd open it later. Rodi slipped it inside his shirt. Folded carefully along its grain, the papyrus followed.

It was time to get out.

Before he could start on relocking the chest, he heard a key in the lock to the office door.

## III

"Didn't need no more keys after all!" one of the men gloated.

"Oh, but get a look at this!" the other said. There was a sound of gold being weighed in the palm of a hand.

"We was told not to touch nothing else," the first man warned. "We takes what we come for, and that's it."

"My arse! I'm having some of this if you aren't."

The first hiding place Rodi had found was under a table covered with a cloth that reached to the floor. Trying not to breathe, he listened to the argument. They spoke the rough Latin of most Italians, though one of them had a slight accent that may have been barbarian. They'd got past the guards outside the Residency. They'd found their way to the Exarch's office. They had keys to the room, and, presumably, to the cupboard and chest. It was a fair assumption they were looking for what he'd already taken.

To some degree the questions of *who*, *how* and *why* overlapped. These could wait till later. For the moment, it was a matter of whether he'd be pulled out of hiding when the men didn't find the documents and went looking through the office. If he did get out of this alive, there was the further question of whether he could get back to the dining room before the Exarch finished his speech, or the slaves came up with the dishes.

He was pulled out of thoughts, half scared, half annoyed, by a sudden obscenity and the sound of a leather bag dropped to the floor.

"Who are you? What are you doing here?" It was Antony. The Exarch's secretary had finally made an appearance.

Another bag fell to the floor. Antony's voice rose to a semi-adolescent squawk of "Help! Help!" before ending in a gurgle that Rodi wanted to mistake but couldn't.

There was a long silence. Then: "This weren't no part of the job."

"Piss off! He was raising the alarm. Let's get the stuff and go."

"Where is it, then?"

More noise, this time of rummaging through gold.

"Ain't here. It might have helped if you hadn't carved up the Greek boy. He might have known."

Somewhere outside the office, a door opened and closed.

"Right, we was told wrong. I'm not staying to get caught." More dull chinking of gold in leather. "You stay if you want, but I'm out of here."

Rodi waited for the whispered bitterness of the two men to go out of hearing. He lifted the cloth and crawled from under the table. The outer part of the cloth was splashed with the blood from Antony's throat. Blood had sprayed over the floor and desk, and lay in a dark pool where he'd fallen.

He'd done with Antony exactly what was needed for the job. But you don't seduce someone and sleep with him every afternoon for a week without feeling some regard. He'd been older than Rodi, but still young and silly. It was a shocking thing to look into his dead face.

Rodi swallowed. He closed his eyes and took a deep breath. He looked at his hands. They were clean. He rubbed his face. He checked his feet. It wouldn't do to leave bloody footprints on his way back to the window. He stood up, and found he was beginning to tremble. He was cold. He leaned against the desk and took another deep breath. Far outside the office door, he heard a sound of shouting, and then a long scream. He'd lost track of where Eleutherius might be in his speech. That no longer mattered. The speech wouldn't be finished. What did matter was getting out of this room before it filled up, getting back to where he ought to be before Cosmas woke and began looking about for him.

His gloves were where he'd left them. He fumbled his way back into them. How to manage the downpipe with these suddenly nerveless arms and legs? The noise of calls and shouting beyond the office and its anteroom was coming closer. Rodi pulled himself together. He'd done his job. Time now to get out.

His last view into the room, before clutching hold of the downpipe, was of Antony's still body, a scattering of gold all about it.

## IV

The crescent of the waning moon hadn't yet cleared the buildings behind him. Unlike the Imperial Capital, Ravenna had no street lighting. With the stars alone to give him light, Rodi stood higher on tiptoe and strained to see into the darkness that lay beyond the city wall.

A dozen yards along the rampart, he heard a faint catching of breath, and a familiar pattern of leather soles on stone. He didn't turn.

"Your leg is still giving you trouble."

Synesius let out a disappointed cough. No longer trying to creep, he limped the final paces that separated them, and leaned with both elbows on the battlement.

"There was a time," he sighed. "Oh, there *was* a time, dear boy." He coughed again. "The idiot monk told me you'd gone out for a walk. I guessed you'd be up here for the solitude."

"I was expecting you."

They stood awhile in silence, looking out. No enemy in his right mind ever camped under the walls of Ravenna. Though they'd started yet another of their sieges, the Lombards kept to the far edges of the swamps that secured the city on its land side. You'd sometimes catch sight of horsemen on the causeway road by day. Other than to speak to the Exarch or one of his underlings, they always kept beyond the killing range of the catapults. Sometimes by night, you'd see a couple of lamps moving about on the causeway. There was nothing out there tonight. The oozing, plopping sounds of the mud were no longer worth remarking – nor was the splash of some night animal through one of the larger puddles.

Synesius cleared his throat. "I got as close as I dared to the harbour. Just to remind us we're sealed in, there are lamps every six foot along the chain." He waited for Rodi's comment. When there was none, he grunted and stood back. "Rotten luck, of course. If things hadn't gone so completely tits up, we'd now be looking at the stars from fifty miles along the Adriatic."

He sat stiffly down. He unstoppered a flask and drank. "Good plan, boy – well-executed too. But there are certain occupational hazards that even the best planning can't eliminate." He drank again and handed up the flask to Rodi. It contained wine of a sort – though spiked with something more powerful than wine. Rodi fought to suppress the burning in his throat.

Synesius tried to move his leg. The injury he'd picked up on the road had settled into a chronic pain. Rodi sat beside him and helped straighten the leg. He muttered a few words of thanks and took more wine. "Completely tits up," he repeated. He leaned against the outer parapet. Another moment, and he sat forward.

"Very well, Roderic," he opened, his voice suddenly firm again, "now we're away from that bloody monastery, and there's no reasonable chance we'll be overheard, I'd like you to take me properly though the whole operation. Try to leave out nothing. I'll be the judge of what's irrelevant."

Keeping his voice low, Rodi went over all that he'd seen and done. He reached the point where he'd scrambled from the downpipe and pulled on his robe, expecting uproar at any moment.

Synesius interrupted. "The little serving room was still empty?"

"Yes, though I could hear slaves carrying stuff up the stairs. I was back in the big dining room before they could arrive."

"And the dining room was unchanged?"

"Yes. Cosmas was still asleep where he stood. Everyone else was where I'd last seen him. The Exarch was getting to the final passage in his speech – the bit where he promises final victory over the Persians. Before he could get into this, someone came beside him, and whispered in his ear. He paused and frowned. Then he shrugged and said something back, before going on with the speech."

Synesius laughed softly. "You were expecting him to jump up with a squeal of horror, and cancel dinner?" He fiddled with his flask. "Eleutherius isn't your standard court eunuch. He can't get children, and has little taste for sex. But he's a competent general, you watched him give that envoy from the Pope a dressing down. However, any other messages after that?"

"No. After we'd finished cheering the speech, he gorged his way through everything put before him, while joking with the Lord Bishop of Ravenna."

Rodi fell silent. Theatrical or muted, the Exarch had still bolted off their escape. Long before dinner was over and everyone was allowed into the wide square outside the Residency, Synesius had watched the raising of the harbour chain. They were trapped within a three mile circuit of walls.

Now he'd finished his narrative, the drugged wine suddenly unblocked feelings Rodi had so carefully put at a distance. He looked into the clear sky.

"I heard them cut Antony's throat." He tried to keep his voice from shaking.

Synesius put a bony hand on his shoulder. "Your job, Roderic, is to lie without passion, and to steal and to kill. The same applies to making gifts of your bottom. Antony was unlucky. He'd have died whether or not you were there to witness it. Taking a professional view of the matter, not having him alive to grass on you from a rack in one of the Lord Exarch's dungeons can't be inconvenient."

The old man was right. In his place, Cosmas would have embraced him, and prayed, and let him cry till there were no tears left. The dry comfort Synesius had given was more effective. Rodi was glad of his company. He'd ignored the plain wording of the Lord Treasurer's warrant that only Rodi and Cosmas were to set out from Philippopolis. He was deserting his post as spy-in-chief of the Slavs who'd settled in Eastern Thrace. The sight of his packing boxes in the cart had annoyed Cosmas no end. Now, if there was anyone who could get them out of Ravenna alive, it was surely Synesius.

Rodi looked at the outline of the biggest church. Ravenna had no street lighting. Behind the church, though, the lighthouse must be in full burn. The port was sealed. But it would never do for any of the Adriatic pirates to run aground.

He had control of his voice again. "I suppose we're in the clear." He paused. "I mean, even if they get caught, no one will believe that those intruders found the cupboard already bare. We do nothing and wait for the chain to be lowered again?"

Synesius tried to get up. His leg had gone to sleep, and it needed all Rodi's strength to help him to his feet and prop him against the battlement. He looked once more into the darkness. "Their silence is undoubtedly welcome. But, if he really wants no one to leave, why hasn't the eunuch lined these walls with guards?"

Rodi listened for the sound of the ever-shifting mud. The breeze from the sea hardly ever fell. If it did, they'd be knocked backwards by the mud's corrupted smell. "You've said yourself the causeway is the only safe approach. Step off it, and sinking without trace is a matter of when, not if. Why bother with the walls when there's a port to be kept closed?"

"Take your mind fully off that dead secretary, Roderic, and *think*." There was a sudden scowl in his voice. It was as if they were back in his teaching room, and he was deep into number theory. "There's no land escape for people like us but along the causeway. For anyone who makes the effort to seek them out, there must be a whole network of paths through the mud. I take it the Exarch must have a description of those two intruders. Why assume they will be trying to leave by sea? Why no guarding of the walls? I could also mention the lack of any obvious search through the town."

Something unpleasant began to crawl into the back of Rodi's mind. "Perhaps they were caught at once. It would then have been obvious that someone had beaten them to the documents."

"Good boy!" The scowl was gone. "Further question, though, is why everyone was let out of the Residency without being strip-searched. Eleutherius has done worse than that when squashing common sedition. To save his own skin, he'd think nothing of slitting every stomach in Ravenna to examine the contents."

Synesius hobbled sideways on his bad leg. When it didn't fold under him, he leaned against the wall. He drank more wine. "Any thoughts on who those men were?"

"The Boss may have other agents in Ravenna. That, or it's another failed Intelligence Bureau operation." Rodi trailed off.

"Think again. Alaric uses only the best. Even the Intelligence Bureau doesn't employ bodgers like that. But they did get in, with keys and a plan of the Residency. We can be reasonably sure what they were after. Wouldn't you like to know who killed your friend, and why?" Like a shift of gears in a water mill, he changed both tone and subject. "The parchment letter's enciphered with a book code. I haven't yet been able to guess the key."

"Haven't we evidence enough?" Rodi's mouth was suddenly dry.

Synesius tittered and burped. He handed over the last of the wine. "Don't worry, boy. I'm not asking you to break into the Exarch's library, to make a list of the unshelved books. I simply don't enjoy looking at anything I can't read. There's already too much here that doesn't make sense." He watched Rodi drink. "Oh, it was a *lovely* plan – lovely on the assumption of a quick smash and grab and run for it. Not so lovely when you find there's nowhere to run."

He leaned on Rodi's shoulder. "Be careful with me on the steps down from here. Cosmas the Thick won't be happy when we roll into his monastery so late and reeking of wine. If I fall and gash my head open, you'll never hear the end of it."

## Part Two – Ravenna, Thursday the 21st September, 618 AD

# I

"Oh, but it's awful!" Cosmas repeated. He struck a pose that upset any balance between his corpulent belly and his knees. He righted himself just in time and raised his voice, not caring who else might hear and understand him. "This is a terrible world. Its end surely can't be long delayed." He pointed at the fresh notice. "Do read it again, Rodi. You know this Latin is beyond me."

Rodi put up a hand to shade the sun from his eyes. It blotted out sight of the empty gibbeting cages. He read into Greek:

*Wanted for questioning. Antony, secretary to His Highness the Lord Exarch Eleutherius. Five solidi paid, no questions asked, for any information that leads to his apprehension.*

He could have skipped the description. But the work of putting one language into another had a settling effect on his nerves. Still pretending to shade his eyes, he looked round the crowded square. Coming off the bridge over the Grand Canal, he'd thought someone might be following them. He'd thought the same as they left the Saint Vitalis Church, and again while Cosmas dawdled outside the gates of the University. Every boatman on every canal they'd crossed over or passed beside had come under suspicion. But no one had been following them. No one was following. A whole morning out and about in Ravenna, for no better reason than to get Cosmas out of his monastery, and they'd had no attention but from the usual mob of traders and beggars.

"What do you suppose he might have done?" Cosmas asked. There was a commotion of many voices by one of the money changing stalls, and Rodi pretended not to hear the question.

What was Eleutherius playing at? Of course, bodies can disappear. One of his first jobs for Alaric in Constantinople had been to help dispose of a Persian double agent whose head had come off while he was being hanged in a brothel. It was possible that someone in the Residency had cleared Antony's body away and blamed him for stealing the documents. But this raised endless further questions he was in no position to even turn over in his mind. Also, though possible, it was unlikely that several pints of Antony's lifeblood had been removed without trace from the soft furnishings of the Exarch's office. By all accounts, Eleutherius wasn't a man easily deceived. He'd had this notice put up in the Central Market in full knowledge of the death.

Cosmas spoke up, as if his normal voice wasn't enough to wake the dead. "Do you think he stole something from the Lord Exarch? Was there a guilty look about him when you saw him before the big dinner?"

Rodi turned away from the notice. A dozen of the city guards were filing into the far side of the square. He fought against rising panic. They were here only to shepherd the latest batch of condemned criminals. He'd read their names and alleged offences on another of the notices. One of them was to be burned without prior strangling, the others merely blinded. He fought harder. The most likely spy really was a drunk. The pool of sick he was bringing up was too convincing even by the Lord Treasurer's standards.

"I haven't seen Antony since Tuesday," he said with a show of indifference. "He was busy all day yesterday with the Exarch's speech. When I did see him, it was only to speak about geometry. Shall we go back?"

Cosmas sagged a little. "Oh must we go back already? Isn't Ravenna just a glorious place in the sunshine?"

"You are the Abbot. You need to spend *some* time in your monastery."

Cosmas looked again at the notice. Given half a chance, he'd launch into an improvised sermon on the text *Forgive us our trespasses*. It would be an excuse to pray over the condemned criminals, and to follow them all the way to their punishment. Given less than that, he'd still do anything to put off returning to his duties.

They'd come so far out of their way to avoid one of the poor districts. Word was that someone there had died of plague. So late in the season, it had to be a fanciful word. And, though fringed by a vast pestilential swamp, Ravenna hadn't known an outbreak of plague in living memory. The breeze from the sea held back the miasma. The sea itself was continually washing out the grid of canals that imposed order on the biggest and the last unsacked city in the Empire's western provinces. Rodi had agreed to the detour only because even more time would have been wasted on a search for the afflicted house, and more again on giving comfort to anyone who might have looked troubled by the proximity of death.

The monk settled into a low rumble of praise for the "missing" secretary, and of warnings about the horrors of temptation. Rodi led him back in the direction of the

Grand Canal. The high, ornamented bridge that crossed it here gave a fine view over the central buildings. Standing there at dawn was said to revive the lowest spirits. Arm in arm with Cosmas, Rodi stared only at the worn cobbles. The Avenue of Perpetual Glory was another place laid out to dazzle the senses. It dated from the time when Ravenna had first replaced Rome as administrative capital of the West, and the Western Emperors needed something to let the world believe they weren't just poor cousins of the real Emperor in Constantinople. No Western Emperor now, just the Exarch. Nor was there much left outside the city walls to be administrated. But the glorious buildings remained, if dulled by lack of maintenance. These too Rodi ignored. For him, the Avenue was a quarter mile of shortcut to a part of the city where neither of them wanted to be. Once they'd passed beneath the unfinished triumphal arch, even Cosmas began to trail off.

## II

A cavernous building, its externals much blackened by centuries of charcoal smoke, the Saint Andrew Monastery radiated gloom at two hundred yards. Once, it had been flanked on one side by a library and on the other by a bathhouse. At some time in the more or less distant past, these and the other surrounding buildings had been bought up and declared redundant and levelled to make gardens for the monks to grow their own food. No food ever had been grown there. Now, the Monastery loomed over an expanse of low bushes and piles of uncleared brickwork.

The man waiting before the main gate was Brother Timothy. His back was turned, but there was no other monk in the Order with the combination of his stoop and the mass of untended hair that hung down from his tonsure. He looked round at the noise their feet made on the gravelled approach.

"What does he want?" Cosmas moaned.

"Probably another complaint about the salt pork," Rodi hazarded. He had no wish to interpret another of their disputes. Perhaps they should have stayed in the centre to watch the punishments.

Timothy hurried forward. "Where have you been all day with the fat Greek?" he snarled in Latin.

Rodi's face darkened. "You will speak with more respect of the Reverend Father."

"*Acting* Reverend Father, if you please." Timothy flashed a sneer at Cosmas. "I've just had it authoritatively confirmed. Clerical appointments in this

Order by the Patriarch of Constantinople need to be ratified by His Holiness in Rome. No letter from Rome, no proper Abbot."

Cosmas watched him turn and make once more for the gate. "It *is* the salt pork, isn't it?" he whispered. He gave way to a sudden flash of ill-humour. "Well, if he and his friends still want fresh meat every day, and no getting up in the night for vigils, you can remind them that this is supposed to be a monastery, not a boarding house for younger sons of the rich."

With rising distaste, Rodi watched Timothy from behind. No doubt he'd be darting inside, to lead out another delegation of noses put out of joint. The size he was, no one could think Cosmas had ascetic leanings. Even by his lax standards, though, the Monastery of St Andrew the Alms-Giver had been in need of reform. Rodi didn't fancy interpreting yet another bitter argument over how the Order's rental income should be used. But, if there had to be a row, better to have it out here in the sunshine.

He was wrong. Timothy stopped a few yards short of the gate. Instead of more like him spilling out to blink in the sun, there was a youngish man in white now on the steps.

"Roderic of Aquileia," he said in the unmistakeable voice of a eunuch, "I must inform you that the Lord Exarch has immediate need of your company. He will not be pleased by the delay you have caused him."

## III

No false beard this time, nor paint on his face, nor any wig to cover his own grey hair, Eleutherius sat behind his desk. With pauses only to sip wine through a glass tube, he was dictating an interminable letter in Latin to the military commander in Bari. Eyes lowered, Rodi stood where Antony had been butchered the previous day. No trace of blood – though the limestone tiles were scrubbed obviously lighter than the others. He resisted the urge to look at the cupboard where he'd found the letters.

Timothy had been triumphant, Cosmas in despair. But he wasn't actually under arrest. An arrest would also have been overseen by a eunuch, but with a couple of guards to make sure he didn't try bolting. He'd then surely have been thrown into a dungeon, with someone to gloat through the bars about what even a light racking would do to a child's body. Instead, the eunuch who did lead him here had been almost polite in his fussy way. "Don't speak till His Highness speaks to you." "Don't look at His Highness till you're invited to." "Don't clear your throat before speaking." "Don't violate the presence of His Highness by spitting." And so he'd continued all the way from one of the side entrances of the Residency till they were in the outer office.

He wasn't under arrest. But this was hardly a social invitation. No point, however, in speculating on what he'd be asked. Better to focus on getting himself into the right frame of mind. He was a low-born subordinate of a Greek cleric who hadn't so far made himself popular in his mission to one of the Empire's Latin areas. Obsequious went without saying. Scared too – though best to be scared within reasonable limits. He should have no sense of having done anything untoward.

How about slightly stupid? Probably not. He was, after all, fluent in several languages, and his stated job in Ravenna was to act as mouth and ears for someone who knew only Greek.

Eleutherius finished his dictation. He pointed at the eunuch who'd brought Rodi in. "Supervise the fair copy," he said in Greek. "If you find any obvious errors in my Latin, or in the clerk's transcription, you are permitted to correct them. Take the message under armed escort to the ship moored outside the harbour chain."

He waved at both eunuch and clerk. "You may leave me."

Not looking at Rodi, he picked up a sheet of parchment and began writing with his left hand in the margin of the text that covered it. Rodi heard a snatch of conversation in the outer office and a closing of doors. Then there was silence. Eleutherius continued writing. Once or twice, he referred to another document.

Not looking up, he spoke in Latin: "You are the boy Roderic of Aquileia?"

"Yes, Sir."

"Then you may be seated. Pull up the small chair beside the table. Since your voice shows a little strain, please serve yourself from the jug of lemon water you will find beneath a cloth on the table."

He waited for Rodi to sit and to drink from the glass beaker. He took up a half sheet of papyrus. "You are

Roderic, born in the ruins of Aquileia about a dozen years ago to Gothic parents. Are you able to tell me exactly how old you are?"

"Fifteen, Sir."

His nose twitched. "I took you for twelve. But no matter." He referred again to his note. "Having made your way to Constantinople, you were at some time unknown to me appointed secretary to Cosmas, the Greek monk who is presently acting Abbot at the Monastery of Saint Andrew. I understand he was appointed as reward for his work among the Slavic barbarians in Eastern Thrace."

He allowed the sheet to fall onto his desk. He switched into Greek. "Even if somewhat older than you appear to be, do you not consider yourself rather young for so confidential a post?"

"The Reverend Father trusts me, Sir. And I can read a book at sight in both Imperial languages, and I have a good head for numbers." Rodi allowed a slight rise in his voice, and a note of pride.

"You are aware that my own secretary has disappeared?"

Rodi lowered his voice again. "Yes, Sir. I saw the reward notice earlier this morning."

The Exarch stared at his note. "I am aware of your relationship with Antony."

Rodi swallowed. Using Cosmas for his excuse, he'd insisted on discretion. Unless Antony himself had blabbed, it was worth asking how word had got out. He'd ask nothing. Instead, he could feel his face turning red. That was as it ought to be.

Two cold eyes levelled on his face. "Did Antony tell you of any plans to leave my service?"

"Oh, no, Sir. We – we said very little. He told me his position, but never explained his duties."

Eleutherius drank more wine. Then he scraped his chair back and stood up. He motioned to Rodi to stay seated. Because they generally run to fat in their middle years, you can't always see from a distance how tall eunuchs can be – something to do with continued growth of their arms and legs after they've been cut. The Exarch must have been five or six inches over six foot. With a brisk waddle, he went over to one of his filing racks. He brought back a folded sheet of parchment.

"This is, you will appreciate, a confidential document. What I want of you, boy, is that you should read it at first sight, first in Greek and then into Latin." He dropped the sheet on the desk before Rodi and returned to his chair.

Rodi looked at the folded sheet. How to play this turn in the game? Should he stumble through the reading, skipping words that ought to be unfamiliar? Should he mangle the Latin? But he thought of the sermon he'd written for Cosmas to read out on their first Sunday in the monastery, and the Latin translation he'd made so the audience could follow it. It was possible the Exarch knew of this. He knew much else.

He decided to play it straight. He opened the sheet and read out a dispatch from the Prefect of Ancona – mostly a denunciation of one of the corn dealers. He read it again in Latin. He ignored the Exarch's marginal note, for the Prefect to be allowed to have the man flayed alive in the corn market. Like the documents he'd found the previous afternoon, it was written backwards.

For the first time, Eleutherius smiled. "A fair start you've had to your education – not bad at all for someone born to a race of nomadic intruders into the Empire. Since, all things considered, Antony may no longer be suitable to remain in his post, I am minded to ask the Reverend Father Cosmas to release you into my service. Confidential secretary to an Exarch – quite a step up in life, wouldn't you agree?"

Rodi's mouth fell open. "But, My Lord, surely there are others with better qualifications than mine?"

Another cold smile. "I shall be the judge of that, Roderic. But you will be aware that even educated Latins nowadays are barely competent in Greek. As for Greeks, most of us acquire at best an oral understanding of Latin. Antony will be hard to replace. If you were not available, a far less regular appointment might be required."

Rodi said nothing. He felt that Eleutherius was finished with him for the moment. He stood and bowed.

"There is no one in the outer office, Roderic. Therefore, you must see yourself out. I will call for you when I am ready. In the meantime, do I need emphasise that, if Antony approaches you, or if you become aware of anything else I ought to know, you will present yourself to the Residency guards? They will have orders to bring you straight to this office."

## IV

There were points on the city wall where Rodi didn't need to stand on tiptoe to look over. Since it was still daylight, Rodi stood at one of these.

There was little to be seen. Thirty feet below, a protective ditch eight feet across was filled with dark water. Beyond that lay another few yards of jagged rocks. Beyond that the swamps began. They spread out, a waste of dreary flatness as far as the eye could see. It wasn't possible to see the causeway from here. Rodi was aware, though, of a conference there over light refreshments between the Lombards and the city authorities. Someone in the crowd lining that stretch of the wall had told him that the Lombards were after a six month truce, to begin with the first autumn rain.

None of this mattered to Rodi. He was watching some leech gatherers at work, about a hundred yards from the foot of the wall. The process, it seemed, was to lay a slave in one of the shallow pools and wait. He was then allowed to stand up, covered in dark lumps that were made to drop off by rubbing with salt. After this, blood still running down his withered body, he was put back into the water. Rodi had watched two entire cycles, and was wondering how much longer the slave could last as useful bait.

Not that this mattered either. What did matter was that the gatherers had marked out a path for themselves. Bordered with lines of powdered chalk, it ran at an angle to the city wall, and overlay a streak of darkness on the mud. From where he stood, Rodi saw how the darkness continued beyond the gatherers, and joined a pattern of other streaks. Did these entirely correlate with areas of solidity? Was their pattern a stable formation, or did it shift about? Could they be seen from the ground? Could they be committed to memory, and followed by night?

Every answer involved doubt. The last involved hardly any. He could see how far out the leech gatherers were. A man has a known shape and size. Nothing else beyond the walls had any basis of comparison. What seemed a few hundred yards might be half a mile. The causeway road ran for about a dozen miles. Was this the shortest route across the swamp?

Rodi thought again. Suppose he were to trace a course parallel with the walls? Once he was on the causeway after dark, he could be on solid ground by dawn. It would then be a question of avoiding the Lombards and any other predators, and getting fifteen hundred miles along the Great Military Road that joined Ravenna to Constantinople.

It wouldn't be much less likely a success with an obese monk and an aged cripple in tow...

He stood away from the wall. It was all useless. There was no escape by sea, and none by land. Was Eleutherius on to him? If he weren't continually fighting a tendency to blind panic, he might be able to say. It was clear beyond reasonable doubt that the Exarch knew Antony was dead. Why then ply Rodi with questions about him?

On the other hand, unless it was possible to grow wings and fly across the swamp, Eleutherius had absolute and unaccountable power. If he thought Rodi had those documents, or just might know where they were hidden, the implements of torture were on almost open show. It made no sense.

Could it be that he simply had need of a new secretary? There were still no spies to follow Rodi about. For all he was rattled in ways he'd never thought possible, he hadn't forgotten his training as a spy.

Even as he thought where to go next, there was a noise of approaching men from behind the closest of the hundred-yard towers. Rodi leaned once more on the battlement. It wouldn't be anyone come to arrest him. If it were, there was nothing he could do about it. Now shivering and on the edge of collapse, the slave was being pushed into the water again. One of his owners was fussing over a leather bucket, presumably counting his bag for the day.

The hairs stood up on the back of Rodi's neck. The men were round the corner and approaching along this stretch of the wall.

# V

"You're a low knob-head – that's what you are!"

"You say that to yourself. I won the game, didn't I?"

"It was *showing* the gold, you fool." The angry man saw Rodi, and lowered his voice. "We lie low and wait for tonight. Once we're out of here, you can do what you like. Until then, it's my neck in the noose as well."

The first man laughed – the one Rodi thought had struck the killing blow: "You know Aripert won't pay dirt for nothing if that's all we takes him. Rope round our necks here, or rope in Pavia. You takes your choice."

Not moving, Rodi waited for the men who'd killed Antony to swagger past him. Even without their own confirmation, they hadn't the sort of voices you'd either forget or mistake. He could see them from the corner of his eye. He didn't turn to see them properly. He didn't need to. Here were the two thugs who'd broken into the Exarch's office the previous afternoon. They'd blundered about, looking for what Rodi had already taken. Before they could ask any further questions, Antony had disturbed them, and they'd cut his throat as casually as anyone else might swat a fly.

Unless you're in the hands of a skilled practitioner, there are torments too awful to be fully known until just after they've stopped. So it was now. A day of stomach-churning panic fell away in the blink of any eye. Rodi clutched at the stonework to keep himself from falling down. Antony's killers were still at large and hunted. One of them was scared the other would give them both away by flashing about some of the gold he'd thieved from the Exarch's office.

Two reasonable inferences. First, they hadn't been stopped as they cut their way out of the Residency. Second, and following from this, Eleutherius had no grounds to believe anyone else had the documents.

And Aripert – who was *Aripert*? Rodi thought of the gossip he'd picked up when briefing himself. Aripert was the Lombard King's younger brother. Pavia was the Lombard capital. Third inference: the killers had been working for the Lombards. Their job was to get the dirt on the Exarch – probably for a go at blackmailing him into military concessions. That or a share of the loot.

It all fitted so easily together.

*Rodi was in the clear.*

Trying to think clearly through the rush of elation, he tapped his head repeatedly against the battlement. Both inferences made sense. He'd been called in for questioning because every possible lead was being followed. Assuming his place had been beside the Exarch, it made sense to ask what Antony had been doing in the office. Had he been working with the men? Had there been an argument in the office that got him killed? Without being there to know what really happened, it was reasonable to wonder what he'd been about. Antony was under suspicion, not Rodi.

*So why the pretence that Antony was missing? Why block off only the escape by sea?*

No immediate need to answer these questions. Eleutherius was bent as a woman's curl. He was in with the Adriatic pirates. That much was clear. What else he was up to could be vaguely imagined, and might explain any amount of freakish behaviour.

What did matter was that no one had any reason to believe that Rodi had been anywhere near the Exarch's office. He was as much in the clear as any of the sailors on the ships bobbing about beyond the harbour chain.

Still arguing, the killers had passed right by. Soon, they'd be round the corner of the next tower. The nearest exit from the rampart was beyond the tower after that. It was here that the city wall became part of the harbour wall. Since this was blocked off as part of the sealing of the port, they'd not be able to continue along the rampart – not, that is, unless there was something Rodi had missed out. Most likely, they'd have to go down two flights of steps into one of the city's dumpier parts.

Rodi could say he'd learned all that was needed. Why take any risks? On the other hand, here were Antony's killers. It was still worth asking what they'd been about. If nothing else, he might find himself able to do them a quiet disservice.

He'd take no risks. Even so, he'd follow them.

# VI

Half-way between the towers on the next stretch of rampart, some of the street boys had a game they played for money. There was an old shrine – far too holy to be cleared from the inner defensive zone – that ended only about ten feet from the wall. The middle point of its sloping roof was about a dozen feet below the rampart.

The idea of the game was for one of the boys to climb onto the low wall on the city side of the rampart, and jump with closed eyes, and to land upright on the roof of the shrine. It usually drew a small audience, and some desultory gambling from which the boys had their cut. With everyone more interested in the conference with the Lombards, there was no audience. But the game continued. Calling out in a dialect of Latin Rodi still had trouble following, they were laying bets with each other and counting and jumping with their eyes closed. Bearing in mind how far it was to the rough ground if any of them fell, it looked a game for lunatics. But some of the boys were bigger and heavier than Rodi, and he'd never seen any of them go badly wrong.

The killers were out of sight beyond the next tower. Time for Rodi to be off the walls ahead of them. Only one way off.

He smiled at the biggest of the boys. "Can I have a go?"

The boy plucked at the cloth of Rodi's tunic. "Go home to your mummy," he sneered. "You'll break your neck."

"And we'll be in trouble," one of the other boys added.

Rodi took the roughened, dirty hand in his own. Now he'd given up on sneering, the big boy had a pretty smile. This wasn't the first time Rodi had noticed him. He squeezed the boy's hand, aware of how soft and girly his own must feel.

"If you don't think I can do it, shall we say odds of ten to one?" He could simply jump without their permission. But their help would be useful. Also, it didn't seem fair to push in and break the rules.

The other boy glanced at the heap of coppers. He shook his head.

Rodi smiled and took off his cloak and cap. He took off his shoes. He looked again at the big boy. He might be his own age, or a little younger. He had the tough prettiness you see on the streets before the realities of life turn boys into broken down men. The breeze from the sea was rising. It ruffled Rodi's hair and played over his bare arms and lower legs. He felt a delicious tingling all through his body. He was in the clear with the Exarch. Following the killers was an act of free choice, not some desperate shift to keep his own body off the rack.

The killers would still be on the rampart. He had time. He took out one of his silver coins and laid it beside the coppers. "If I do it and live, that against half your pool."

The big boy stared at the silver disk. He looked more annoyed than impressed. Then he nodded. He picked up Rodi's outer clothes and dropped them to one of the boys who was waiting on the ground far below. "Try to think you're jumping into the harbour," he said.

Rodi climbed onto the low wall that bounded the city side of the rampart. He looked down at the roof of the shrine. The ten foot gap would have been a lot to clear if it hadn't been so far down. It was a question of lateral and vertical motion. The extent of the former would be a product of the latter. In his mind he drew a circle. He divided it into sectors. He narrowed the angles. He squatted and jumped forward. He was still thinking of arcs and central angles when he landed upright on the roof.

It was no great triumph, but he was in the mood to think it so. He turned and bowed to the silent boys on the rampart. The big one had his arm stretched out in a gesture of praise. Rodi was in a mood to be pleased. He was pleased. He jumped from the roof to the shrine's lower portico, and let himself down to the ground. He took his clothes from the boy there.

"Wait for your money?" the boy asked. "Or go again?"

Not looking up from his shoe laces, Rodi shook his head. "Tell your big friend I'll be back later."

## VI

The season was still hot enough for the siesta to be kept going. The time of day was deep into siesta. Keeping abreast of Antony's killers was an easy game to play in these dead streets. Outside the central grid of the city, they seemed at first glance as irregular as a heap of earthworms laid out on a paving stone. But they were nothing compared with the poor districts of Constantinople. It was soon better than that. One look at the sun, and Rodi was compiling the streets into a draft map. Give or take a few deviations, they resolved themselves into a series of concentric curves, going inward from the line of the city walls, with smaller bisecting streets.

The killers had left off arguing, but their continued bursts of low conversation were enough to keep them in range. For an amateur, following a man involves shambling along ten paces behind, with a dart behind anything convenient every time he seems about to look round. For Rodi, it was enough to keep an eye on their stride and their general behaviour as they turned into one street, and then to hurry ahead of them along a roughly parallel street, and to watch them go by, forming an updated view of how far they were from where they wanted to be.

He kept with them all through the poor district, and across the intersection of two canals, and into one of the commercial districts that bordered the main port. The streets here were wider and more commodious, and several were lined with palm trees. The windows in the high buildings were all unshuttered, but most had their blinds pulled down. Following the men through one of the empty squares meant having to show himself. But neither looked round. They were now plainly coming to their destination. Their pace was slowing, and one was beginning to look with more attention at the picture signs at the entrance to every side street.

With some dithering, and a show of renewed argument, they stopped by the arched entrance to one of the smaller alleys leading off from a street itself barely wide enough for a single cart. Rodi watched them go in. He waited. They didn't come out again. He waited more. Still nothing. He hurried forward and glanced through the arch.

As he'd expected, the little street was a dead end, terminated by a low building without external windows. There was a porter sitting in the shadow of the open door. There was no getting inside for Rodi. But he could wait and see what happened next.

"It's a knocking shop."

The voice came from behind. Rodi wheeled round, knife in hand. He steadied himself and put the knife away. "What are you doing here?"

## VII

The big boy from the ramparts offered a lop-sided smile. "You must be a right thickie to follow those men. Not a pot to piss in between them. Deadly if they'd seen you." He stood away from the arch. He looked though it to the brothel. "It has dancing cripples in the evening, and drugged beer. I can get you a deal with the owner if you want."

He'd followed Rodi through a mile and a half of silent streets. No one followed Rodi without being spotted in the time it takes to sharpen a pen. Yet he had followed Rodi, and could probably have got him from behind if that had been his purpose. That deserved some respect. It deserved a lot of respect.

Rodi looked at the purse the boy had in his right hand. "You can keep the winnings." The boy smiled again. Rodi shrugged. "What's your name?"

"Scruto."

*Scruto* – a funny sort of name. Not that *Roderic* was anything a civilised man would choose for one of his children.

The boy tucked the purse inside his tunic. "They found me in the rubbish," he said. "It pleased them to call me after it." As if expecting laughter, he frowned. Would he respond with a punch on the nose, or by walking off?

Rodi said nothing. He glanced left through the arch. Nothing doing there. But it made no sense to stand here gossiping. He'd lost those men for the moment. It would have been good to know something about them. Better to find out how they were proposing to get out of Ravenna.

But he'd lost them, and it was best to give way to the reality of that.

He moved out of sight from the brothel. He took his cap off and ruffled his hair. Scruto watched him. "You aren't a Latin," he said thoughtfully. "You're too light for a Greek. Are you a barbarian?"

"What's it to you?"

"Only asking. What's *your* name?"

"Rodi." He held out his hand. Scruto took it. He looked carefully into Rodi's face.

"That was a good jump. You don't scare easy. Nice following too." Rodi managed a dismissive smile. Scruto continued staring into his face. "A man I know is putting a team together. We need someone who can work on the inside. No contact after, except to divvy up the takings. Plenty of the yellow stuff if you want in on it."

Slowly, they walked back in the direction of the big street where two canals merged. It made sense that gambling his neck for coppers was only a bit on the side for Scruto. Housebreaking was altogether more profitable. Almost a pity Rodi couldn't be in on the big job he had in mind. How to refuse the offer without scaring him off?

Before Rodi could think of an answer, there was a noise of murmuring. It came from round the last bend before they reached the big street. Even in siesta, this should have been crowded with merchants, come to haggle over the barges of produce unloaded from the docks. The docks being closed, it ought now to be as silent as everywhere else in Ravenna.

This would be his answer. He put his cap on again. "Come on," he said. "Since you've managed to follow me all the way here, you might as well let me buy you a drink."

## VIII

Long before the hooked bargepoles could take hold and pull it onto the land, Rodi could guess what had been found. The salt water had cleaned and gone some way to pickling Antony's naked body. Very white in the sunshine, it had lost the power to shock it had possessed in the Exarch's office. Or it had lost the power to shock Rodi. The crowd it had drawn thought otherwise. Bodies couldn't be that uncommon a find in the canals of Ravenna. But one of the boatmen lifted up the arms and showed how soft the hands were. That got a general groan of horror.

Scruto looked away from the cleaned gash across the throat. "He was one of those bastard Greeks, I'll bet you," he whispered. "They'll be after the killer. You don't kill Greeks in this town and get away with it." He took Rodi by the arm. "I'm not sticking around for the city guard. It'll be questions till after dark. It might be arrests."

Rodi pulled free and edged a little closer. He'd been wrong about the body's lost power to shock him. The snarl of death washed away, now smooth and pale as fresh marble, it was Antony's face and not Antony's face. In life, it had changed expression and colour almost every moment they'd been together. He'd been a silly young man – his head stuffed with idiot poetry in a language so old Rodi could barely follow it. He'd actually spoken of love – love after a dozen furtive couplings in a disused privy. In the normal course of things, he'd have finished his time in Ravenna, and gone back to Constantinople, to be sent out again to a more exalted post in the Empire's service. Instead, his drenched, naked body lay still on the canal path, an object of passing interest and of pity.

It was also an object of profit. Five *solidi* offered. Five to be earned. Someone called out the Exarch's name. A couple of smallish men hurried forward and knocked one of the boatmen aside. They grabbed the body by its feet and began dragging it along the path. More men appeared. They took the shoulders and pulled in the opposite direction. The idle chatter of the main crowd was overlaid by a calling of obscenities and threats.

Rodi shut his eyes and took a deep breath. Dead was dead, he told himself. The thing scraped back and forth across the paving stones was no longer Antony. There was nothing to be had from waiting here for the city guard to roll up and restore the peace. Better to go back to the monastery. He could sit with Synesius over something strong, and try to puzzle out the workings of the eunuch mind.

But Scruto had him by the arm again. "Did you know him?"

Rodi shook his head. He looked at the street boy's dirty hands and scuffed fingernails. He looked at the mop of dark hair. Though uneven, his face was a pleasing thing to look at. Scruto was alive and warm, and friendly though felonious.

He put the dead body out of mind. "Let's get away for here," he agreed. "I said I'd buy you a drink.

"You decide where."

## IX

Brother Timothy gave him a sour look. "You can't have been with the Lord Exarch all this time."

Rodi wiped the happy smile from his face. "Piss off, Timmy. Try it on with me, and I'll get you a penance of ten lashes every day till Christmas."

Timothy bared his rotten teeth. "Then you'll have to wait for the fat Greek to come back from his own *interview* at the Residency."

That took the wind from Rodi's sails. Timothy noticed. He sidled round, to block the light that came through the monastery gate. "You know, *I* grassed you to the Exarch's men." He turned and pushed the gate, so only a sliver of the late afternoon light came through. "Poor dead Antony – he came here on Monday, to ask for you. I guessed then what the pair of you were about. I call it disgusting! And what would the *Reverend Father* think – him all holy and self-denying, and his boy giving his own body to the filthy vice of Sodom?"

Rodi hurried deeper inside the monastery. Timothy's voice followed him along the main hall: "Throat cut from ear to ear, if I'm told right. Dumped in a canal too. I wonder who it was wanted him dead. *Who wanted that tongue of his stilled forever?*"

# X

Speaking in his slow, accented Latin, Synesius dictated from memory, translating out of Greek as he went:

*"That each individual thing is one and the same with its essence, and not merely accidentally so, is apparent, not only from the foregoing considerations, but because to have knowledge of the individual is to have knowledge of its essence; so that by setting out examples it is evident that both must be identical. But as for the accidental term, e.g. 'cultured' or 'white,' since it has two meanings, it is not true to say that the term itself is the same as its essence; for both the accidental term and that of which it is an accident are 'white,' so that in one sense the essence and the term itself are the same, and in another they are not, because the essence is not the same as 'the man' or 'the white man,' but it is the same as the affection."*

He paused for a long swig from his beer mug. "Any questions?"

Silence. Two of the boys in the classroom stared at each other. Another gave an obviously despairing look at the stick Synesius kept beside him.

He opened his mouth to speak again. Then he caught sight of Rodi's face in the doorway. He finished his beer and stood up. "But, my dear boys, I seem to have kept you far too long. You just run along and think about today's lesson." He turned his mouth down. "I'll have some questions of my own the next time we meet."

He waited for the boys to finish running from the room. He sank back into his chair and began fiddling with his beard. "Do shut the door, Roderic, and sit down. You may already have heard it, but I have some rather bad news for you."

It was nothing the boy hadn't just been told, or that hadn't already gone repeatedly through his mind.

Rodi was first to break the silence that followed. "He *may* have forgotten what I told him about my real job. It was half way up that mountain in Thrace, and we were about to be sacrificed to that idol. He had other things on his mind then. He's never mentioned it since. Cosmas never remembers anything if he doesn't keep discussing it. He *must* have forgotten."

He stopped again. His statement was self-refuting trash. He took another sip of beer. It had something in it that made him want to sneeze. He tried to focus on the two killers he'd seen earlier, and the inferences that flowed so naturally from seeing them. But it was a house built on sand. It still seemed reasonable for Eleutherius to believe the killers had his documents. But he also had his eye on both Rodi and Cosmas. The moment he got Cosmas to blurt out that Rodi was other than the best secretary he'd been able to find in Constantinople, there'd be a eunuch knocking on the monastery gate again. This time, Eleutherius would insist on the whole truth – and his insistence was unlikely to be gentle or wholly unsuccessful.

Synesius refilled both cups. "Rather than listen to me, I'd like you to explain why you have to get out of here alone. Please try to show a better understanding of things than those pig-stupid Latins have of Aristotle."

"Neither of you is up to travelling fast," Rodi began, stating the obvious. He thought. "If we stay here together, we can be disappeared. The eunuch can take back his documents. He can kill or torture us to his heart's content. If he's ever recalled to face questioning in Constantinople, there will be no evidence of his collusion with the pirates, and nothing to connect him with our disappearance.

"However, if I get clean away from Ravenna, he'll not dare lay a finger on either you or Cosmas. Once I'm out of his reach, he might as well regard the documents as already with Alaric. He can still cut a deal when recalled. But he won't hurt you. The worst he might do is try to use the pair of you as bargaining counters. Everyone knows Alaric looks after his own. He won't dare hurt you."

"Oh, excellent, Roderic, *excellent*!" Synesius leaned back in his chair and beamed his approval. "Such concern for the fate of two old men – one of them born useless, the other going that way faster than he'd like." Without warning, he bumped his chair down and leaned forward. "So, how far can you trust the *friend* you picked up in the streets today to help you out of the city tonight?"

Rodi pulled a face. He'd spoken with Scruto purely in the abstract. The boy had told him it would be easy enough to get out. All things considered, he'd probably have said he could help fly Rodi to the moon. "Unless you have a less insane plan, I suggest we have no other option than to find out."

"Then you'd better leave now." He slapped a purse onto the table. Rodi knew how much it contained. He'd helped fill it on their first evening in the city. "Take the low window at the back of the monastery. Once out of

Ravenna, get yourself to Rome. The Exarch may not expect you to head straight into Lombard territory. He also has little power there. Pass through Rome to Ostia. Take ship for Carthage. Though it's late in the sailing season, you should be there in ten days. The Exarch of Africa hates Eleutherius, and will do nothing to stop you. If need be, take him into your confidence. But try keeping out of sight. Another ten days at sea, and you'll be in Corinth. One of Alaric's Jewish bankers has his office there. He'll get you back to Constantinople.

"Until then, we'll see if His Highness the Exarch of Italy really is the cautious player all common sense tells us he is."

There was a loud knock on the monastery gate. Someone not far outside the teaching room cried out in exultation.

Synesius finished his drink. He stood up. He reached for his stick. "No time, dear boy, for embraces, or heroic farewells. I'll hold them up in the corridor. If we don't meet again, try to remember this as an occupational hazard."

## XI

Biggest risk of all – but nothing else for it. Rodi took out the oiled packet. He pushed it though the rusty bars. "Hold onto this. Don't get it wet."

With his right keeping himself steady, Scruto held the packet in his left hand. "Take a deep breath," he repeated. "Go down as far as you can. Come through belly up. Don't try any other way."

The water in the excess canal drain was cold. Because of its salt, it was rather slimy. It also made swimming down and keeping down harder than expected. But Rodi managed on second effort to find the place where two of the bars had sheared off. He felt one of them scrape across his bare chest and stomach, before he could use it to push himself a few inches deeper.

He was through. He was outside Ravenna. He relaxed and was carried straight up the four yards or so to the surface. No coshing from Scruto before drawing breath – no making off with the purse or the packet he'd been handed. Instead, the street boy helped him from the water and sat him on a brick ledge.

The commotion on the walls seemed louder than before. He dried himself on his cloak and pulled his clothes back on.

"Keep your face down," Scruto whispered. "Keep your hair covered." He waved at the pool of light from the torches that began a few yards from the city wall. "Just follow me, and don't ask any questions."

Poking a stick into the soft ground as he went, he led Rodi forward at a right angle from the wall. This was the time of greatest risk, and Scruto did his best to force the pace. They were a hundred paces out before anyone could bring up mirrors to deflect the glow of torches outward from the rampart. Looking back, Rodi had sight of a dozen spots of light playing over the ground they'd covered. One of the spots came rapidly forward, till it reached a few feet from where he crouched. But they were already past the extreme limit of what could be seen.

More poking with his stick, then Scruto took a sharp right. Another dozen paces, and they turned diagonally left, before joining a path that curved outward from the wall.

"Keep hold of me," he said, now in darkness. "One wrong step, and you may be gone before I can pull you out."

They continued in silence across the immense but invisible flatness of the swamp. Rodi looked back once more. The city was already a mile away, its wall a blaze of moving lights. So far, no one seemed to be following them. Perhaps no one seriously believed he'd be able to leave Ravenna without hanging a rope ladder from the battlements. Getting a mile across a swamp was nothing compared to the barely conceivable distance he had yet to cover before he could swagger into the Lord Treasurer's office in Constantinople. But it was a mile farther than anyone thought he could get, and that was all that counted at the moment.

Scruto stopped. The sounds of the swamp rose all about them. He took another step forward, and stopped again. He turned slightly left. "Why did you kill that man?" His voice was suddenly cold.

"Who says I killed anyone?"

"Everyone says you killed the Exarch's secretary. I saw how you looked at the body. Now, you're running away."

More inferences – this one as sound as any Rodi had made. "I haven't killed anyone, Scruto. But would you wait around and trust in the Exarch's justice?"

Scruto grunted. "It doesn't matter either way. I'll give you a choice. I can take you right across the swamp. But there's no telling if we can get there by daybreak. Or I can take you to the causeway. If there are no Lombard patrols, you can be twenty miles away before the dark goes. It's your risk. You choose."

"I'll take the causeway." Rodi's boots were already heavy with the stinking mud. He had no doubt Scruto knew his way, but the dread of stepping so much as an few inches to right or left of the safety of an unseen path was a growing and omnipresent force in his mind. He looked back once more at Ravenna. It reminded him of a city taken by storm and set alight. There was no chance, out here in the darkness, of seeing the causeway. But it couldn't be that far away, and the absence of lights moving along it surely counted for something. If he got a move on, he could be out of reach before anyone realised he'd left the city.

He was wrong about the distance to the causeway – that, or the route chosen by Scruto was more oblique than he'd imagined. It came finally in sight without warning. One moment, they were squelching across a flatness honeycombed with pockets of corrupted air. The next, Rodi found himself not a dozen feet from the raised bank of the road that joined Ravenna to the rest of Italy.

Standing on the causeway, he had enough light from the stars to see along the road. To know they were at the fourth milestone from Ravenna needed him to run his hand over it like a blind man over a face. He stood up. He turned to Scruto, five *solidi* in his hand. "This is where we say goodbye."

Scruto stared at the dull shine of the gold. "Keep your new-minted gold, Rodi. I'd be arrested the moment I tried to spend one of those." He cleared his throat. "Can't I come with you?" He stepped forward and put a hand on Rodi's chest. "Why not carry on together?" His voice took on a tone of open pleading. "Don't make me go back to Ravenna, Rodi – please."

The offer made a little sense. The Exarch would eventually send out a search party. It would be looking for one boy, not two. Also, if Scruto had never gone beyond the far limits of the swamp, he knew more of the language and ways here than Rodi did. He was big, and he must know how to fight. Rodi might be able to draw on his barbarian origin. But he'd been too long in schools of one kind or another, and too long thinking mostly in Greek, to pass as other than a complete outsider.

He stood away from Scruto. "No. What I'm doing must be done alone." Now they were out of the swamp, the normal difference of rank was restored. He spoke with the firmness he'd heard when Alaric refused a petition. It was natural he should worship Alaric. It was natural too that he should see Cosmas and Synesius as something like close relatives. But he was already slipping into an affection for Scruto that was in no one's interest.

"Go back to Ravenna. I'll send word when I can."

Scruto knew his place. It was painful to watch him go slowly down the bank and disappear into the gloom. Rodi was sending him back to a worthless life in Ravenna. His best luck would be to mess up a jump from the rampart, before he could get himself tied to one of the Exarch's wheels, for breaking as a thief.

Rodi waited to see if he'd come back to plead again. The boy was gone. He took a long step forward along the causeway. Solitude was the life Rodi had freely chosen. He'd never been a child. He'd never be a youth.

## XII

The moon came up as he passed the ninth milestone. Its glow was too sickly to show anything of what lay either side of the causeway. Its light was barely enough to show how the dust was lifted from the road and moved about by the sea breeze.

At first Rodi had broken into a gentle trot along the road. The greater the distance he put between himself and the gates of Ravenna, the less uneasy he felt. But the clatter of his feet had itself become a cause of unease. After a few miles, he'd slowed again to a walk. It made no difference. No one was following him. There would eventually be the Lombards to face. They would be clustered about the far end of the causeway. But they weren't looking for him. They weren't expecting him. He could slip through the Lombards. After that, he could take the road south. His idea was to attach himself to a group of pilgrims. He'd blend in and only detach himself when the walls of Rome were in sight.

So far, he'd been kept going on what Synesius called the boundless reserves of youth. He'd been awake, though, since shortly after dawn. He could keep going till the next dawn, and some time beyond that. But he was growing weary. He was cold. Though the days continued warm, each night was chillier than the last. He still hadn't warmed up from his soaking in the canal. He was hungry. He was thirsty.

Where and how long to rest? The second answer was easy – he'd keep his head down till it was dark again. Where to hide by day had to depend on what he found once off the causeway. Burned-out monasteries were never far off any road he'd known.

A night bird flew past behind him. He stopped and looked nervously round. He didn't see the bird. Now he was still, he was more aware of the belching sound from the surrounding swamp. Ravenna had vanished to a spotty blur on the horizon. He was alone on the causeway. He was tired. He was cold. He was hungry. Above all, he was scared. The sooner he was away from here, the better he'd feel.

He set out again. It made sense for the Exarch to put out word that he'd killed Antony. It justified the frantic search he'd seen put up in the streets of Ravenna. As always, the problem was the timing. Cosmas had been called in. It was easy to imagine how he'd told Eleutherius everything he needed to know. But that would have been after Antony's body was dumped in the canal. Why put it there unless Rodi was already to be blamed for the murder? At every step, the Exarch seemed to be responding to events simultaneously or in advance.

A thought crept into his mind. It was so outrageous, he pushed it out again, unconsidered. He was tired. Any amount of nonsense drifts through a tired mind.

The packet of documents was stiff against his chest. It was sealed, and he'd kept it dry. Outside Egypt, though, papyrus was delicate stuff. He'd need to make sure it didn't come apart on the long journey ahead. He tried to cheer himself by thinking of the look on Alaric's face when the packet was opened. The fantasy didn't involve emptying several dozen fragments onto the Lord

Treasurer's desk that needed to be gummed to a linen backing.

*The journey ahead!* Synesius had made it seem the easiest thing in the world. Rome, Carthage, Corinth, Constantinople – every one of them half the Empire apart. Until he was outside the Exarch's reach, he'd be hunted like a wild animal. Even beyond the Exarchate of Italy, Eleutherius might be willing to hire private assassins. Or there were bandits, or pirates, or shipwrecks. Or there was the time involved. Synesius had given the best sailing times. He'd made no allowance for bad weather or delays in port while booking his place on the right ship. If he was in Constantinople by Christmas, he'd be lucky….

Rodi was aware too late of the tripwire his left boot brushed against. Before he could pull himself together, he was stumbling forward. He recovered his balance too late. Though he darted forward, he still had no speed when the net was thrown over him. Its lead weights brought him down. Every effort he made to get free only tangled him in it more hopelessly.

"Where's your purse, you little bleeder?" one of Antony's killers rasped into his face. "You don't move an inch if you want to keep a tooth in your head." A knife went to his throat.

Somewhere behind an uncovered lamp, the other killer let out a cry of warning. "Hang on, hang on! He's the one what they was looking for." He laughed. "Don't you put no mark on the boy. The Lord Exarch won't pay for damaged goods."

## XIII

"Sit down, Roderic." It didn't look as if the Exarch had stirred from his desk since their last meeting. Though dawn still hadn't arrived when he was brought in through one of the Residency side exits, Rodi was dazzled by the glow of a dozen wax candles.

"It's shuttered and locked. No chance of a quick suicide. No chance of another shimmy down the pipe. So please sit down, and do help yourself to a cup of wine. You'll have to trust me it isn't poisoned. Try to bear in mind that I want to speak to you as one servant of the Emperor to another."

Rodi stared at the opened packet before the Exarch. He struggled to pull himself together. He'd never beg for mercy. It would do him no good in any event. "Servant of the Emperor?" he managed in a faint croak. "Pirate King, more like!"

Eleutherius raised his eyebrows. "The difference between a pirate and an emperor, Roderic, is mostly one of intention and scale. Both must do things the squeamish don't wish to think about. If you prefer to stand, you may. If you won't drink, I will." He reached for the jug and poured himself a full tumbler. No longer the boring, hieratic speaker of the previous afternoon, no longer the closed, suspicious bureaucrat of their last meeting, the Exarch seemed to be enjoying himself.

They were alone in the office. Rodi had been untied before he was brought in from the outer office. He was tired. He was bruised all over from the journey back. His legs were beginning to shake again. He was scared he might start to cry. He sat down and poured a drink. It was more honey than wine, but would moisten his throat.

"Why am I still alive?"

Eleutherius unfolded the sheet containing his account of monies received. "Because I didn't order you to be killed. Wouldn't a more useful question be when and how I rumbled you?"

"Would you answer it?"

"Probably not.

"Are you hungry?" He lifted a cloth to show a plate of bread and honey. He watched Rodi eat.

Afterwards, he picked up the silver bell beside his inkstand. The door opened and the same eunuch as before came in.

"I think we're ready for the entertainment." The eunuch bowed and went out again.

Eleutherius got up. "You may remain seated, Roderic. But turn your chair about. This is as much for you as for me." He went and stood in the middle of the room. The squeaking of wheels Rodi had already heard became louder.

One after the other, two wheeled chairs were pushed through the door. They were parked either side of the cleaned spot on the tiles.

"I trust you recognise these men, Roderic?" He walked to a point equidistant between them. "You'll agree this is where they murdered him?" Bound and gagged, one of the men who'd killed Antony began twisting his head. His fingernails dug into the arm of the chair. The other went into a snuffling scream through his nose.

Eleutherius leaned over the first killer. "Did you *really* think," he asked, soft and sinister in Latin, "that I'd believe your story? Did you think I'd reward you for bringing in the blond boy?"

He turned to Rodi, still in Latin. "My normal preference is for something more theatrical than the bowstring – lowered into a bath of molten lead, flayed or burned alive, fed to hyenas: you get the idea." He smiled sadly. "But these things take time to arrange, and my domestics are already unnerved by what was done to poor Antony."

He bowed to the large man who now came into the room. "Try not to sever any blood vessels. Limestone is such a nuisance to clean afterwards. But make it quick. This is more about tidiness than display."

Devoid of feeling, Rodi watched the men die by strangulation. He watched as the bodies were wheeled out, still upright in the chairs. He watched Eleutherius walk lightly back to his own chair and drink more wine.

Rodi let it show that he was suppressing a yawn. "Now you've killed your first set of agents, I suppose you'll want me to deliver those documents to the Lombards."

He couldn't help himself. The draining away of apprehension was too much. Watching the Exarch spill wine down the front of his tunic gave him his first laugh in days.

## XIV

After the wine he'd drunk, Eleutherius bordered on the jolly. "Of course I was annoyed you climbed up here, and that you got to the cupboard first. You'd buggered months of preparation. But I soon warmed to the possibilities you'd opened. The problem with all operations of this kind is the mode of delivery. Though I'd made sure to keep in the background, there was the chance those men wouldn't convince the Lombards. Letting you escape, on the other hand, gave the documents ideal provenance. I only had to tip off the Lombards once you were out of Ravenna, and wait for the desired result.

"I wasn't pleased to be woken and told you were back in Ravenna. On reflection, I probably should have had some lead warmed for that pair of idiots."

Rodi yawned openly. "And what is the *desired result* of letting the world know how bent you are?"

"Not as bent as the documents claim, Roderic. For the rest, running an Exarchate without anyone to tax does compel a certain irregularity of supply." He gathered the documents together. One of them had cracked along its grain. "If His Magnificence the Lord Treasurer Alaric doesn't always take you into his confidence, you can hardly complain if I won't. But, unless you can think how it will be to my personal benefit, you'll have to take my assurance that getting these documents into the right hands will be to the benefit of both Italy in particular and the Empire in general."

He stood up. "Come with me, boy." He led the way across the room, to a table behind one of the filing racks. It was covered with a map of Italy.

"In formal terms, the Empire holds about a third of Italy, including a strip of land connecting Ravenna to Rome. The reality is that we hold these coastal areas in the north and these regions in the south. The rest has been taken by the Lombard invaders, or has no overall control. Rome itself is effectively governed by His Holiness.

"Some years ago, the Lombard King changed his title to 'King of All Italy.' We organised a shout of laughter through all the other barbarian kingdoms. Last year, when their new king repeated the claim, I scraped an army together and laid siege to him in Pavia. His mother persuaded him to go quiet on the claim. Young Aripert, his brother – young, but sharp beyond his years – joined in the urging.

"I could have stayed under the walls and scared them into a formal renunciation. But the money ran out, and my army deserted.

"Worse than that, with every passing year, the claim acquires greater prescription. Though its capital has been moved to Constantinople, the Empire began in Rome and with the conquest of Italy. The no doubt temporary loss of Egypt and Syria to the Persians is something we can bear. The total loss of Italy to a race of barbarians whose fathers used to tattoo their faces would be a more sensible humiliation."

He returned to his desk again. He went through a stack of documents and found the warrant appointing Cosmas to his monastery. "I take it for granted you forged this.

Your friend the monk is not the most intelligent of men. But there is a discrepancy with dates that means it had to be a local production." He pushed it across the table. "It's a very good forgery, and you had no choice but to juggle the dates. I mention it only because the failure of my second attempt to get those documents into Lombard hands has given me time to widen my ambitions.

"There are things I want you to carry to Pavia for getting into the right place. There are other things you must commit to memory and produce on the spot."

Eleutherius had managed some sleep that night. Rodi was ready to drop. But he stood up straight. "And if I refuse to get involved in your dodgy and still unexplained schemes?"

The Exarch smiled. "Well, I could write a letter of complaint to Alaric. Bearing in mind, however, the slowness of the posts, I must instead threaten to have Brother Cosmas put into molten lead. The agony will be both prolonged and exquisite. When he has stopped screaming, I will have you put in beside him. The idea, by the way, is to place a victim gently on the surface, and let his weight carry him in."

He picked up his bell again. "But you must forgive me, Roderic. Your friend is in the outside office. He is most touchingly concerned for your safety. Before I send you off to bed for the night, nothing will more delight me than to be the cause of your happy reunion."

## XV

It was the following night. Rested, bathed, fed, briefed, promised on a stack of relics, provided with all necessary things, Rodi stood beside the little eunuch who, for the moment, had taken over as Antony's replacement.

"When I open the side gate, you run for it. Don't stop running. If anyone's looking, you need to make it clear that this is an escape. Do you understand?"

Rodi had been through the plan more than once with Eleutherius. He didn't need some underling to remind him. Not looking at the eunuch, he nodded. "The walls have been cleared?"

"We've laid on a night execution. The Lord Exarch has found someone to impale. The walls should be empty – but keep up the pretence, even so."

A mile along the causeway, Rodi slowed to a brisk walk. Another half mile, and he sat down to re-lace his boots. He'd been aware some while of the soft padding of feet behind him.

"What's the price on my head tonight, Scruto?"

"Fifty *solidi*."

"I'm worth every ounce of it, and more."

"So why were you taken from the Residency and allowed to get away?"

Rodi had known they were followed to the gate. "Is there anything I can say to make you go home to your bed?"

"I've never had a bed."

"Then stop asking questions. You'll get no answers, and they'd do you no good if you did get them."

He let Scruto help him to his feet. Arm in arm, they set out along the causeway.

**Part Three – Pavia, Monday the 25th September, 618 AD**

# I

Now the rain had left off, it was back to the remnants of summer. Rodi squeezed himself forward in the jostling, cheering crowd for a better view of the procession. In a sudden blare of drums and trumpets, he watched the men at arms pass by, then the priests. By the time the people of quality were through the old triumphal arch, the sun was drawing clouds of steam off the road.

It didn't matter. He could see enough to imagine the rest. There was young King Adalward, clutching at himself and giggling in the first carrying chair. Immediately after, pious behind her veil, his mother had eyes only for the unfinished church they'd come out to inspect. Beside her on horseback, General Sundarit was doubtless looking fearsome and annoyed – fearsome on account of the knockout blow he had in mind for the Exarchate of Italy, annoyed to be taken away from planning it.

But even half-finished, the Church of the Holy Virgin was the largest building in Pavia, and the grandest ever commissioned in one of the barbarian kingdoms. All other business had to be secondary to the semi-*impromptu* service of thanksgiving at seeing the main dome fully in place. The common people were delighted. The Catholic and Arian Bishops had left off arguing over whose church this was to be, and were standing at the same height on the steps to receive the royal party.

Scruto poked Rodi in the side. "You might at least keep back in the crowd."

No arguing with that. But Prince Aripert was now through the arch – Aripert, the brains in the family. Antony's killers had been led to believe they were working for him. Not speaking, Rodi strained to see his face. He failed. Once more, though, he could imagine it – all the glum resentment you'd expect in a younger brother who fancies the crown for himself.

There was no arguing with Scruto. There was nothing to be seen. The day before, barely an hour into their stay in Pavia, Rodi had watched the same cast gathering for the Sunday service in another of the new churches. He'd already put faces to the names in the reports he'd scanned in Ravenna. He should be back in the fleapit of a lodging house he'd chosen for its closeness to the main gate. He'd told Scruto this would be a quick mission. If it was to be that, there was still preparatory work outstanding. Moping about in the open, almost asking to be seen, was at best a waste of time.

A sudden breeze cleared away the steam. With a little discreet help, the King was helped down from his chair. The Queen Mother to one side of him, Sundarit the other, and Aripert behind them all, he shuffled towards the foot of the steps. The Bishops came down together. To avoid any show of precedence, there was no kissing. After much synchronised bowing, they joined into a single party and hurried up the steps to vanish inside the cavernous and as yet unrendered and unpainted interior. After a polite interval, the crowd streamed forward into the square and formed a queue to be let in to join the service.

"Are we going in too," Scruto asked. He was getting angry. He was right. Though different in their purpose, intelligence work and housebreaking were games with overlapping rules. The most obvious common rule was to keep out of sight.

Rodi shook his head. The tavern gossip that morning had been all about the wrangling between the two churches over a service that neither would regard as giving in to the other's heresy. The final agreement was that the Creed would be interrupted at the critical moment by a shout of "Praise be!" while the priest covered his mouth. It would be anyone's guess whether he defined Christ as "one with the Father" or "like unto the Father." A shame no one had thought of that before. It would have cut out three hundred years of argument and saved as many acres of papyrus. But Rodi could think of no excuse for seeing how this went.

He stood back to make way for an old woman to hurry for the church. "Let's have another look at the Palace."

## II

After a childhood spent in the rubble of Aquileia, digging for scraps of iron for beating into simple tools, Rodi had fallen easily into the general prejudice of the Empire, that whatever the barbarians took they made into a desert. Pavia was disproof of that. Of course, nothing compared with Constantinople. Ravenna, though past its best, must be the finest city in the West. But Pavia remained a grand place of baths and churches and wealthy houses. The shops and markets were more bustling than those of Ravenna. The Lombards, it seemed, had destroyed nothing after their initial conquests. Now, with their almost manic building of churches, they might be improving on what they'd found.

They were even popular with the natives. The guards for the royal party had been entirely for display. Some people in the crowd had thrown flowers. Here, in the renamed Alboin Way, the longest street in Pavia, most of the shopkeepers still had pictures on display of the last Lombard King.

None of this concerned what Rodi was here to do. Even so, it added to his general sense of disquiet.

The Royal Palace was at the western end of a circular space with a high victory column in its centre. Rodi had read the pompous inscription on its base, put there by an Emperor whose name was new to him. He'd been more struck by how the column's height was one third the radius of the ground space, and much more by how its shadow was used to record the time on different sets of bronze numerals in the pavement. According to the numerals for the present month, it was now the third hour of the day – some time yet to go before lunch.

He stood before the gates of the Palace. The new object he'd seen while pacing along the shadow of the column was a parallel text in Latin Greek and Lombard. The rain had made its ink run like mascara on the face of a hired mourner. One look, and his spirits had risen. Explained in private, it would improve Scruto's mood. Theirs would, after all, be a quick mission.

"You looking at something, boy?" Rodi had seen the guard from the corner of his eye. A big Lombard squeezed into a silvery breastplate, he looked just the sort for idle gossip.

"What's it say?" Rodi asked in halting Latin.

The guard's response was a doubtful look. Rodi's tunic was covered in stains, and he'd lost weight on the journey across Italy. He didn't look at all the sort the author of the notice could have had in mind.

Rodi tried to look winsome. "Please, Sir, tell me what it says. I never learned any reading."

The guard stroked his dyed beard. "Why my lad, it's an open invite to anyone who can put on a show for His Majesty." He jabbed a finger at the Greek version. "There's a big feast on tomorrow. Everyone who's anyone will be there."

"We're jugglers and dancers," Rodi said. "Does that mean we can come?"

Someone behind him laughed. "I hardly think so!"

The guard stood up straight and saluted. He looked about for the sword he'd put down. "Bow to the King's brother," he growled to cover his own surprise.

Either the service had been cut short, or Prince Aripert had dodged out of it. His ceremonial robe put off, dressed now in the clothes of a wealthy Latin, he stared at his polished fingernails. "The last time I saw the list, we already had fire-eaters and some Jew hovering above his grave who says he can make nails stick to a piece of stone. I don't imagine you can do either of those." He turned to Scruto and gave him a slow inspection. "I don't suppose you can dance and juggle on a tightrope?"

Rodi tried to click his heels together. "No problem, Sir," he said brightly. "Tightrope dancing is my brother's speciality." He stepped on Scruto's foot. "When do you want us here tomorrow?"

Not looking at Rodi, Aripert smiled. "Rope dancing, eh?" He put out a hand and moved Scruto's face to right and left. "Rope dancing – you might do very well for that!" He walked round the boy, looking at him from all directions. If the King was sixteen, Aripert couldn't, as a younger brother, be older than Rodi. But, though still beardless, he had a large and powerful frame.

What else to expect? His complexion shouted *I'm a barbarian*. Within living memory, his grandfather had burst from the mountain passes into Italy, face covered in tattoos and quite as ferocious as the Avars. No one might think that now, to see such fine clothes, and hear such smooth, unaccented Latin. No one might dare to remind him. But that's what he was. Rodi was small even by Greek standards. Aripert was every inch a barbarian of the higher classes – doubtless all the more dangerous for the veneer of civility.

He took a few steps away from Scruto. "Listen for the beat of the big drum from that tower over there. You'll be let in through the side entrance in Swyving Lane." He nodded to the guard. "See to it they are let in."

Ignoring the guard's salute, he looked at Rodi. "You only get fed if the King likes you." He looked again at Scruto. "But I don't imagine that will be a problem."

## III

Paint too little water on the backside of a papyrus sheet, and there's no visible effect. Too much, and the glue is all washed away and the fibres come apart. Rodi held up his third effort. In every sense, it looked better than the others. Running from right to left, and slightly downhill, the script exactly produced the scruffy yet pedantic style of the Exarch. Holding it by the corner between forefinger and thumb, he carried it to the window. He set it, written side to the sun, on the drying rack he'd improvised.

Behind him, with a soft thud, Scruto fell once again from the rope he'd stretched across their room. Rodi looked round. He was wrong. This time, he'd landed on his feet. Rodi still frowned. "I've told you there won't be any rope dancing."

Pleased with himself, Scruto bowed. "If Aripert says he wants rope dancing, it's rope dancing he'll want."

Rodi thought of a curt reminder that there were guests in the room underneath. All this jumping on the boards might get someone banging on the door. Instead, he pursed his lips. "I promised it because we need to get into the Palace. We shan't be staying long enough to risk our necks."

He left Scruto to his balancing and turned back to the letter he'd forged. It was plain that reading would have to be in a mirror. But, as with the ageing process, he was less sure about the substitution cipher he'd used. Make it too easy, and the letter might be rejected. Too hard, and the Lombards might not be able to read it.

He swore and snatched at the sheet. He'd applied too much water. It was supposed to curl the papyrus before it stiffened again, not soak through to the ink. He dropped it onto the pile of other sheets set aside for destruction. He sat once more at the table. He pressed both hands together. He cleared his mind of everything but a vision of Eleutherius behind his desk. He sharpened his pen. Keeping it in his left hand, he dipped it in the ink he'd specially prepared. For the third time, he wrote in cipher text:

*"Your threat, my dearest Sundarit, displeases me. If you are mad enough to publish the documents you claim to possess, I will make a full and sufficient denial. I shall also find myself with no choice but to make your people aware of the treasons you have committed against them. Recall, for example, the nature of your dispositions at the battle of Castellone. Would you have it known exactly why you allowed me to withdraw with minimal losses? Please, therefore, desist from further threats of this nature. As a token of my continued regard for you, and in hope of our continued agreement, I have directed another hundred pounds of gold to be credited to your account in Naples."*

It looked sufficiently damning. It incriminated without going into details that would themselves be suspicious. Adding to it the documents he'd first seen in the Exarch's office would close off any defence that this was an Imperial production.

He thought. Sundarit was literate. He'd seen samples of his writing – an easy hand to copy. But was this one of those details that went too far? Probably not. Rodi put his pen down. He picked up another in his right hand. He dipped it in lighter ink. With much pressure that spluttered ink as he went, he wrote in the margin: "Worthless fat bastard!"

He turned the sheet sideways, and then upside down. It looked convincing. If he changed his mind, there was time for another go later.

The banker's draft, made on parchment, he'd produced the night before. This had been the weakness in his outline plan. Being caught on the journey over with the original documents would have been a nuisance, but would only have required him to move to the less devastating Plan B. Caught with anything else, and he and Scruto would have been dragged into Pavia for hanging on meat hooks in the sun. Even so, the banker's seal couldn't be produced on the spot. He'd had to carry that, stitched inside the collar of his cloak.

He looked at the draft. The lead seal had been used – used and scraped as clean of detail as the silver coins he was using, and pushed six inches into the earth of a flowerbed on the far side of the Lombard capital.

He realised that Scruto was staring over his shoulder. Unlike Sundarit, the street boy was illiterate. That had stood to reason. Rodi, of course, had checked for himself. He'd lived too long now in a world where things were seldom what they seemed to take anything on trust. But, unless he was the sort of agent Alaric would have snapped up on the spot, Scruto was illiterate.

He cleared his throat. "So this is what will get the Lombard General killed?"

Before Rodi could answer, there was a knock on the door.

## IV

The owner of the lodging house tried to push the door open. The wedge underneath it, and Scruto's full weight from the inside, kept it three inches ajar.

"You gave my doorman a bad coin!"

He was a lying turd – him or the raddled old pimp he employed.

Rodi focused though the gloom of the passage at the bleary face of their landlord. He looked at the outstretched hand, in its palm a lump of copper washed with silver. It was nothing he'd given at the door. But he'd not argue.

"I've got a better one. Hold on."

He slammed the door shut and bolted it. He went over to the purse he'd left beside the bed. He fumbled through it for something that was undeniably genuine, but not suspiciously so. "Get ready for when I open it again," he muttered at Scruto. With all the papyrus and inks he'd set out, the room was like a scrivener's workshop. One look inside, and he'd never get rid of the landlord.

He opened the door again. "This is the only one I've got till my uncle arrives."

The man took it and gave it a bored glance. He moved closer to the door and tried to see past Rodi. "This is a respectable house, I'll have you know. There'll be no funny dancing on my floors."

"Oh, indeed not, Sir!" Rodi smiled. The man's garlicy breath would have made a dog vomit. "As soon as my uncle arrives from Milan, we'll be moving to a bigger room. He always carries good silver."

After another attempt to see into the room, the man gave up – though probably only for the moment. Rodi shut and bolted the door. He poured a cup of unmixed wine. It was filthy stuff, but it slowed the pounding of his heart.

Scruto laughed. "Should have let him think we were a pair of thieves. He'd have given us a better dinner than he did yesterday." He bent over the forged letter. "So will this do the trick?"

Hands still trembling, Rodi put the letter beside the Exarch's account of monies received. There were slight variations between the papyri used. But there was no reason for both documents to be in exactly the same condition.

He'd have to give some kind of answer. "Politics in the Lombard court are difficult to follow," he opened after another mouthful of wine. "Sundarit and the Queen Mother head opposing factions in the military sense. He wants to clear us out of Italy while we're up to our necks in the war with Persia. She wants peace with the Empire, and even cooperation against the Avars. At the same time, they appear to be lovers. Or they once were lovers. The King usually does as his mother tells him, but doesn't like her nagging about his taste for sex and sport. Aripert is the clever boy in the family, but has no foreseeable chance of becoming more than uncle of the next King.

"Get them into the right place, and these documents might take Sundarit down. All we need, though, is for his knock-out blow in the south of Italy to be put off till the spring. By then, the Franks will have been bribed into invading from the north."

Scruto yawned. He went and sat on the bed. "So, why have you been told to tip off the Queen Mother, not Aripert? You've been sent all this way, and for what? Chances are she'll just sit on everything."

Nothing they hadn't already discussed. Nothing Rodi could answer. Should he try another sneer at Aripert? On the way back here, that had got Scruto's mind off everything else. Not a good idea, though. He picked up his stack of waste papyrus. He tapped the sheets together. They were almost the same size. "I've been told what to do, and I'll do it," he sighed. "The wider issues aren't our business."

Scruto leaned forward to poke at one of the waste sheets. "Tell me if I'm missing something, Rodi. I know I don't have your education and what not. But let's have another look at this. The fat eunuch isn't trying to drop Sundarit into the shit. He's trying to pull him in beside him. There may be something really clever here that I can't see. But, even if this lot isn't meant to come out, isn't he taking a risk? I don't believe your friend the Exarch gives a toss about the Empire – not enough to risk his own place in it. So what's he *really* up to?"

Rodi looked away from the mocking stare. "I'm doing this to get Cosmas out of the eunuch's web. That's what *I'm* up to."

"And you think he won't kill both of you?"

"Though I can't risk doing it, I'll tell him I've sent a letter to Constantinople. That will get him playing by the rules."

A feeble answer. He turned back to the business in hand. With a sharp knife and a ruler, he sliced the sheets along the grain into half inch strips. He turned them about a right angle and cut them into half inch squares. He dropped them into a pot of beer vinegar. Before they set out again from the lodging house, the squares would have swollen to a mass of disintegrated fibre. The pot could be emptied into one of the street privies that he'd choose at random. He'd get rid of the ink and the pens as well.

He reached for the folded parchment he'd taken from the Exarch's office. The neat block of Roman numbers, separated by dots had disturbed Synesius on first inspection. It added mightily now to Rodi's disturbance. Reveal the text its author had used as the key, and each number would turn straight into a letter. In principle, content analysis of the numbers should allow guesses to be made about the meaning of the more frequent numbers. But Synesius had tried this for Latin and Greek and Lombard, and all the various Germanic and Slavic languages he and Rodi knew between them. The cipher text had remained a mystery. He'd tried the more obvious arithmetical progressions. In the time available, he'd still drawn a blank.

Why give this to the Lombards? They surely couldn't be up to cracking it. Were they aware of the key text? He looked hard at the first line of numbers. This might be in pure book code, and give the progression used to hide the rest. But none of the numbers were repeated – no clue to its meaning. He looked again at the seal. There had been two, the second placed over the first. The wax couldn't be separated to show what the first had been. The second was carefully effaced.

Scruto gave up on questions that he knew couldn't be answered. "When are we going out?"

"Soon enough." Rodi refolded the parchment. He recalled what Synesius had said when they were together on the walls of Ravenna: *There's already too much here that doesn't make sense.* He put the parchment into the flat leather sleeve that would eventually contain the whole set of documents.

One thing did make sense. Whatever else he was up to, Eleutherius had Cosmas glued fast in his web. Only that counted. The Empire could go hang. Its affairs were nothing to Rodi. Duty to Alaric was the guiding star of his life. But the nature of that duty was presently unclear. And so it was duty to a shambling old bear of a monk. Unless Rodi did exactly as required, Cosmas would never be let out alive. Even if he did the job, it might not be enough. But there was enough difference between *might* and *would* for Rodi to keep going.

He gave a final glance at the leather sleeve. If only Synesius were here as well. But that was too much to ask. He could be glad the old man had somehow limped away from the eunuch in time, and that he might still be hidden away somewhere in Ravenna.

Scruto lay back on the bed. Guessing at the time, Rodi looked out of the window.

## IV

Like Ravenna, Pavia had no street lighting, nor was there any moon to supply the lack. By day, the street where Sundarit had his house was crowded with pedestrians and carrying chairs. Somewhere far off, a dog was barking. Here, the only noise was of a few chirruping insects. Another few nights of this cold, and there'd be no insects.

Rodi pressed both hands against the dim outline of the wall. The only window on the outside of the house was on what had to be the third floor. This was barred and probably shuttered and bolted.

"A challenge," he'd said on their inspection after lunch. "A challenge," he whispered now.

"Piece of piss, more like!" Scruto's rough hands made a scraping sound on the wall's rendering. Now that it was his turn to do something, he was almost cheerful again. A pity it was too dark for Rodi to see the first practical demonstration of his talents.

"No sign of a break-in," Rodi reminded him, "not so much as a mark with your fingernails."

Silence.

Rodi waited. Scruto wasn't close by him. Perhaps he was feeling his way about the circuit of the wall …

He stepped aside just in time to avoid being hit on the head by the end of the rope dropped from above.

"Come on," Scruto called softly. "It'll take your weight." He laughed. "Bet you'd like to know how I did it!"

It was the question uppermost in Rodi's mind. He'd ask it when he had more time, and when he was over the shocking loss of face. It was for something like this he'd brought Scruto along. He hadn't realised what an amateur he'd find himself by comparison. The rope alone must weigh as much as he did. He took his shoes off. He tested the rope. As fast as he could without kicking against the wall, he pulled himself up forty feet to the roof.

He didn't acknowledge Scruto's warning about loose tiles. Not making a sound, he was first to the ridge tiles, and first to look down into the blackness of the courtyard.

The stars told him that north and south ran diagonally across the building. He called into his memory the plan of the house drawn by one of the previous Exarch's spies. It was a largely conjectural plan, and five years old. If it was correct, Sundarit had his office on the first floor of the block on the far side of the courtyard.

Back to the ridge tiles and two balancing acts till they were in the right place. In no time, Scruto had the rope hanging down about a foot to the left of the greater blackness of the window.

"Still no chance in your head this is a set up?"

"No *reasonable* chance."

Scruto sniffed. "Then I'd better go down first." His voice didn't allow for objections. Rodi looked again. He could make out the window sill. Alone, he'd have no trouble. By why object? If he peered hard enough, he might learn from an expert.

Scruto went down with one hand on the rope. He stopped exactly level with the window, and rocked himself onto the sill.

Rodi tested his weight on the lead of the gutter. He leaned forward for a better look.

Then: "I can't get in, Rodi. There's a padlock."

Rodi smiled in the dark. Oh, what a crestfallen tone that had been! "Stay where you are. I'm coming down."

It needed both hands to get at the lock. Scruto had to hold him steady. But it was a simple mechanism. With a soft click, it was apart in a dozen heartbeats. Still in Scruto's arms, he pulled one of the shutters open. They both listened. Beyond reasonable doubt, the room was empty.

Rodi sat down, his legs inside the room. "I go in first. Don't follow till I say."

Holding onto the window frame, he lowered himself an inch at a time. His toes made contact with wooden boards. He lowered himself farther, till he was standing in the room. He bent slowly forward and moved his outstretched hands about. No lengths of twine stretched low on the floor to give the alarm. Probably no security beyond the padlock. Still feeling about as he went, he moved deeper into the room. He found the door. It was locked. A few feet along the wall, he made contact with a padded chair. He sat in it and reached inside his tunic.

"You can come in now. Close the shutter and keep still."

Rodi uncovered his glass tube. He'd filled it the night before with the brightest glow worms he could find this time of year. Eyes closed, he shook them into more active life. He lowered the tube and smiled at Scruto.

"I'll bet your housebreaking friends never thought of this!"

Giving at best a feeble glow, the worms were enough to get them the layout of the room. The plan he'd seen was wrong. This wasn't the office. It was some kind of filing room. Against one of the side walls, a single rack was stuffed with various documents. Near this was a long table spread with maps. One of them was a detailed plan of Ravenna, marked with what looked like paths though the swamp.

"But doesn't that look nice and full?" Scruto pointed at a purse being used as a weight to hold one of the parchment maps open.

"And if it is?" Rodi thought of his first visit to the Exarch's office.

Scruto heard the alarm in his voice. He was quietly amused. "Difference, Rodi, between a thief and execution fodder is knowing when and when not to steal something. I won't be lifting the General's purse." He moved beside Rodi. "But don't you feel the buzz – being in someone's house, that is?"

"No." Careful not to move it, Rodi leaned over one of the smaller maps. It was of a small city, and showed the high and low places in its surrounding areas. The writing at the bottom was too small to see in the light available.

"I used to know someone who couldn't hold onto himself," Scruto continued in a low but excited whisper. "Always had a dump where he broke in – smeared it all over the walls. Sometimes stripped off altogether and got into a bed ..."

Rodi stood up straight. He shook his tube, till the glow was as bright as it would ever be. "How long did he last?"

"Not long. I saw him roasted over a slow fire outside the house where he was caught. But doesn't this do *anything* for you?"

"I've told you it doesn't. We're in. We do the job. We get out. We take nothing. We touch nothing."

In the silence that followed, Rodi listened for any hint of movement elsewhere in the house.

Scruto stood back from the table. "So where are you planting the General's death warrant?"

"Under that, I think." The nude statue had given him a momentary fright. He'd been warming to it ever since. The documents had to be hidden but findable, though not by accident. Where else but under the statue base?

A rapt look on his face, arms about its waist, it took all Scruto's strength to tilt the stone figure an inch forward from the wall. Rodi slipped the package under its base. He had his fingers free just in time as it swayed back into place. He heard the soft crackle of squashed papyrus. So far as he could tell, the position of the statue looked unaltered. It might not have been moved since before the Lombard conquest, when this must have been the house of some rich nobleman. If the Queen Mother chose not to do Sundarit over, it might not be moved again till the house was demolished.

But none of this was Rodi's concern. The first part of his job had gone without a hitch. It was time to cover his glow worms and get out.

The room was empty again, nothing apparently touched. He'd already clicked the padlock shut, when Scruto suddenly froze beside him.

"Shit! Shit! I said it was a set up!" Another moment, and he was up the rope and climbing over the parapet. "Come on!" he urged.

Rodi looked round. On the far side of the courtyard, there was a waving about of lights behind one of the sets of shutters.

# V

Presumably, it was Sundarit speaking. "Let's cut the diplomatic smooth talk, Gregory," he rasped in good but accented Latin. "You turn up outside the city gate at God-knows-what hour. Then with a change of clothes, but no bath, you come straight here to scratch on my door. You don't do any of that unless your friends in Rome want something, and want it urgently. So, shall we start again?"

Scarcely breathing, Rodi shifted position on the window sill. He took one hand off the rope and pulled himself noiselessly along the shutters till he could see more through their central gap. His fingers were like ice. His ears and nose were tingling. His breath, when it came, showed as steam against the chink of light.

Here was the office, and it was filled with the light of two big candles. Sulky in his dressing gown, Sundarit leaned forward in a chair that creaked under his weight. On his feet, cup of wine in hand, the Papal Envoy was in his full official rig.

Scruto plucked again on the rope. This time, Rodi didn't look up at the dim shape leaning over the parapet. He pulled on the rope and went back to squinting back and forth through the crack to see if the two men were alone.

The Envoy was moving about. "I do grant, dearest Sundarit, that the hour is late, and I am most grateful that you were willing to receive me in private. Of course, this is a matter of some urgency, and *not a little delicacy*."

Unbidden, he scraped a chair across the floor and sat down, out of sight. There was a rustling of cloth and a slight bump, as of a wine cup placed on the floor.

"Without beating around the bush, my dear fellow, His Holiness has thought again of your kind offer, and is now unable to accept it. I can only suggest that you call the whole thing off while you can."

Sundarit moved again in the chair. "*Call the whole thing off*, Gregory?" he asked with slow menace. "Call it off, six whole months after it was agreed? We've agreed you can have the new church. We've agreed to declare for the Catholic Faith, and tell our Arians to roll over or get lost. We've lifted the blockade of Rome. We've agreed to give you everything you asked for." He sniffed. "What bribes has the Exarch been handing about in Rome? They must be bloody whoppers!" He switched out of Latin for something poetic and obscene in his own language.

It was almost possible to hear Gregory spread his arms. "Look, Sundarit, my job is simply to pass on messages. I'm as upset by this as you are. But I have to inform you that, if you go ahead with your winter campaign, the southern bishops won't declare for you. That leaves you with a choice between retreating and having to fight your way to Bari. Are you aware that the Frankish King is ready to withdraw his envoy from Pavia?"

Sundarit laughed. "I'd like to see him dare a northern attack in the winter."

"Oh, but haven't you heard that His Majesty is already gathering an army on the border? If you march south, he can be under the walls of Pavia in a week?"

Sundarit got up. For a moment, Rodi thought he'd come over to fiddle with the shutters. Instead, he went out of sight in the opposite direction.

There was a noise of rustled papyrus. "Anything else to tell me?"

"Nothing, my dearest friend – except to express the most heartfelt felicitations of His Holiness."

"Last information I had from Rome, Adeodatus was sick in bed, covered in disgusting boils. You write to the clerical ticks who run policy in Rome. I'll see you out of the house."

Rodi waited till the door was opened and closed, and the sound of retreating footsteps was out of hearing. He pulled hard on the rope, to make sure it was still firm. With a flourish, he kicked himself away from the wall. Just as he swung back, he was level with the parapet.

"Well?" Scruto was angry, and he was scared. In his line of work, this was a disaster barely avoided. Rodi kissed him on the cheek. For him, it was a glorious and revealing bonus. He'd finally had his "buzz".

"Interesting," he said, now trying to keep his voice neutral. He looked down into the darkness of the courtyard. He could have slipped and fallen. The rope might have broken. He might have made a noise and been discovered. In place of that, he'd got answers to one or two of the questions that had nagged him since before he was off the causeway from Ravenna. If another had been raised, he'd see if he could get that one answered too before the dawn.

He beat Scruto to the ridge tiles. "Come on. I'll give five to one he's not going straight to bed.

# VI

Without flaring torches to light the way, the Envoy travelled slowly in his carrying chair. It made following him along Alboin Way slightly harder than if the guards and carrying slaves had been too dazzled to see outside their own pool of light. But slightly harder was much less than impossible, or even difficult. Like pack animals stalking their prey, the two boys hung back a dozen yards, each in the deeper shadow of the high buildings.

The Envoy's party came to a bisecting street. It turned right, towards the central baths. Before reaching that cavernous building, there was a turn to the left, and then another right. They were now in the street where craftsmen unpicked silk cloth imported from the Empire for spinning into lighter fabrics. Drifting from another street came the unmistakeable smell of a soap manufactory.

There was a slight movement ahead of blackness on black. "A fine evening, my Lord Gregory," a voice said in Greek. "But haven't your carrying slaves had enough exercise?"

The Envoy laughed. "Trying to stop my dodgy heart, are you?" He climbed from the chair and muttered something in Latin to his slaves. They moved to the far side of the street. "You always were a wicked boy, Aripert."

They walked together back along the road. Rodi pressed himself into a doorway and held his breath while they went past him. Not moving, he waited for them stop and begin whatever conversation they had in mind.

They stopped beside a small church, and went under the cover of its entrance. Rodi walked slowly after them, till he came to another recess. He went inside and listened hard.

"Do you think you put him off?" Aripert asked anxiously, in fluent Greek.

"I still don't think it was wise to lean on him," Gregory answered. "He's been rumbling on about his invasion for two years. He's done nothing yet. Isn't he supposed to be laying siege to Ravenna at the moment?

"I did as your mother asked. But I may only have jogged his arm into doing something."

"You haven't seen the proclamations he's been sticking in front of my darling brother to seal." Aripert controlled his voice. "His Majesty spent every day last week trying on suits of armour. He's stopped listening to Mummy. The brainless bag of lard's even threatened me with a monastery if I don't shut up about peace with the Empire. Sundarit has him like a child's toy. All we can do is load up the costs of actual war."

Gregory let out an impatient groan. "I've done everything I can, Aripert. The rest has to be up to you and your dear mother. We can't afford any trouble – not this year, not next. It's in none of our interests to have the Franks on the rampage in the north."

He moved into the street. "It's worse than that, however. Just as I was leaving Rome, I got a letter. Because you won't believe its content, I'd better let you read it for yourself." He hurried past Rodi to his chair. He came back, now with a covered lamp in his hand. Rodi watched him disappear into the doorway of the church. With a noise of unfolded parchment, a pool of dim light spilled out into the road.

"Oh, Jesus!" Aripert was aghast. "God's bloody tits!" He dropped his voice. "What are they up to in Constantinople? Can't they just sort out the Persians?"

"Word in Rome is that the Persians have messed up in their occupation of Egypt. There's effectively a ceasefire on all the other fronts. The Emperor has time to waste on Italian affairs."

Aripert read again. "It means either we back down at once, or we make sure to win in a single campaign." The lamp was dimmed.

"I don't like the sound of the second," Gregory said in a nervous whisper. "The Franks *are* on the warpath. All they need is a bit of subsidy to bring them through the passes into Italy."

"Then leave it with me." Aripert's shadow stepped briskly into the street. "The letter changes everything. Can I hold on to it for the moment?"

He laughed under his breath. "Yes, leave it with me, Gregory. I think I can find a way to kill several birds with a single stone."

They both walked past Rodi again.

# Part Four – Pavia, Tuesday the 26th September, 618 AD

# I

Without the thick bank of cloud overhead, the sundial might have shown the second hour of the day. The numeral for September glittered through a puddle nearly a yard across. Both the cold and the colour of the cloud promised more rain.

Rodi was wearing his worst shoes – soles thin as papyrus, and a hole under the ball of his right foot. His cloak was better quality, but third or fourth hand, and it had lost most of its original dyed colour. The effect was between plain beggar and someone who was trying to look as unbeggarly as he could afford.

He'd been woken at dawn by the beating of rain against the shutters. He'd washed and dressed and, once the rain stopped, had come out alone. Scruto had been right about the effects breaking and entering could have on the spirits, and would probably sleep far into the morning. An hour of walking through thinly-peopled streets, then a long stay inside a baker's shop, with beer and a pasty for breakfast. He should have put himself on a bench under one of the colonnades, or stepped inside one of the churches. Instead, it was back to the circular space before the Royal Palace. He'd never thought about sundials, but there were always mathematics behind their construction. The use of a perfectly vertical column for the gnomon had required much compensation in placing the hour markers. The designer had used a double formula. Reasoning back to this had so far defeated Rodi. That didn't mean he'd give up.

He looked at his reflection in the puddle. He could see that his eyes were too far apart as these things were judged. He couldn't make out the dusting of freckles. If they'd appealed to poor dead Antony, they didn't appeal to him. Nor the narrow shoulders. Nor the ribcage slightly too large for the shoulders.

Thoughts of himself turned into thoughts of Aripert – not the shifty politician he'd spied on in the night, but the smooth, well-made youth he and Scruto had seen here the day before. He had the same colouring as the Prince. He was about the same age. But it was useless any more to think that Nature would grow any kinder in his approach to manhood than when he was a child.

He looked up to watch a line of carrying chairs go through the palace gates. His orders were to tip off the Queen Mother. That meant getting close to her. In turn, that most conveniently meant turning up at the feast. Of course, instructions to an agent in the field always included some allowance for local facts. The Exarch had said he wanted Sundarit neutralised. More important, that was his obvious interest. Now Rodi knew what he did, wouldn't it make better sense to get a letter to Aripert? Rodi had seen him wandering about earlier, an abstracted look on his face. No guards as such, but he'd been followed by a small army of flunkies. All of these must be illiterate. Slip one of them a letter – preferably in Greek – and it would surely be passed on. By the time he had the General under arrest, Rodi and Scruto could already be outside Pavia.

But, though the small details would be uncertain, Eleutherius knew the political contours. He'd specified the Queen Mother, not Aripert. The Queen Mother it would have to be.

Trying not to show what he was about, Rodi began pacing out the distance from the highest of the December numerals to the column. Unless he could track her down to one of the churches, getting to the Queen Mother meant another day in Pavia, and much of the late afternoon behind the gates of the Palace.

His mood should be bordering on the jubilant. He couldn't yet cry "Mission accomplished". Even so, last night had gone as smoothly as one of the acrobatic acts he'd seen in the Hippodrome. For what it was worth, the conversations he'd overheard would make a nice report. Creeping up on Aripert's veiled mother was little by comparison.

But it was obvious why his mood was falling. So long as he was taken up with the how and why of the Exarch's orders, he could leave aside thoughts of the future. This time, come next morning, he'd be twenty miles outside Pavia. There would be questions he had to answer – questions without easy answers.

He stared at the inscription on the base of the column: *Placed by the Municipality of Pavia to celebrate the everlasting glory of the Lord Emperor....*

A voice cut in from behind him: "There is, dear boy, a simple verification of hyperbolic declination lines on a sundial. The distance from the origin to the equinox line should be equal to the harmonic mean of distances from the origin to summer and winter solstice lines."

## II

Synesius brushed more crumbs from his beard, and reached for his wine cup. "Oh, the story, Roderic, would fill a book, and there isn't time for writing one. I spied out the generality of what you'd been sent off to do. I got out of Ravenna, and then I hobbled after you. I'm not yet a complete invalid, nor yet a dotard."

He turned to the Jewish tavern-keeper and spoke in one of the Eastern languages. The man bowed, hurrying off with the empty jug. "Fine people, Jews," he added under his breath. "They don't ask questions of each other, and never grass to the authorities. I've often found it useful to pass as one of them."

Rodi went back to the main subject. "So how do you expect to slip a letter to the Queen Mother?"

The old man raised his eyebrows. "Don't ask such questions, my lad. You're pretty good, I'll allow. But I'll do the job with greater finesse than you've ever shown."

They waited for the tavern-keeper's boy to place the new jug on the table. Once he was gone, Synesius refilled their cups. "What I told you at our last meeting still holds. I want you out of here before noon, and on the road south to Rome. Don't stop till you're in Alaric's office. There's something odd going on in Italy. What you saw last night gives no answers, but only raises more questions."

"And Cosmas?"

Another lifting of eyebrows. "If your monk isn't dead already, he'll surely live till he bursts from overeating.

I'm not your superior as such, but I will remind you of your duties."

"And how will you get out of here afterwards?"

Dry laughter. "One of your strong points, Roderic, is that no one looks twice at an unprepossessing boy. Mine, I regret to say, is that no one would dream of suspecting a broken down creature like me. Give me the message you've prepared. I'll see it's delivered. And I'll get out alive. The way you often dawdle about, I may be in Constantinople before you."

Rodi finished his wine. Light-headed, he stood up. "I'll go and gather my things."

## III

The landlord blew his nose into the palm of his hand. He licked at the snot. "They came for him just after you went out. Most upset your *brother* was. He cried your name, but went willingly in the end." He wiped his hand on the front of his tunic. He held it out, palm up. "Now, if you'll please, there's a little matter of unpaid rent."

Rodi looked about the room. He'd cleared out anything incriminating the night before. Little of their own stuff had remained after that. Of this not a shred was left in the room. The floor had been swept in all the easy places, the stained bedsheet pulled into place. It was as he'd found it the day before last, and as the next guest would find it.

"*Who* came?"

The hand curled back on itself, before straightening again. "Now, that would be telling. I run a respectable house. I don't want no friction, if you know what I mean." His thumb and forefinger rubbed together. There was a gloating look about him, and it wasn't the anticipation of treble rent.

Rodi stepped backwards through the door. Before the landlord's thuggish doorman could make a lunge, he'd taken the first flight of stairs in a single bound. He dodged under the pair of arms that reached out from an open door, and made it down the next flight.

There were three men waiting in the tiny hallway. He turned to make for the back door. This led to a patch of courtyard garden. Beyond this was a secondary gate that was usually open.

The gate was closed. By the door another man stood. He was tall and powerful, his blond hair arranged in elaborate plaits, a club in his right hand.

"You are under arrest, Roderic of Aquileia," he said with only a trace of a Lombard accent. "If you resist, I have orders to pacify you with this. If you manage to get away, I have further orders to carve the face off your Latin friend, before gelding him."

Rodi heard footsteps approaching from behind. He'd already reached inside his tunic. He took out his knife, and threw it, still sheathed, to the floor.

The Lombard nodded at one of his men to take the knife. "Can I take that as your agreement to cooperate in full? It would be most useful for us all if I could make that assumption."

Rodi let himself be pushed into a room without windows. It had a filled bath, beside that a suit of clothes made from what appeared to be white silk.

"Afraid the water's cold. But His Highness the Prince Aripert is only lending the clothes. He wore them when he was ten, and they still have a certain sentimental value. He wouldn't want them covered in stains."

## IV

Not hungry, Rodi turned his face away from the dish of baked meat set at his end of the table. He lifted the wine cup he was sharing with his captor – "Grimald," he'd been called by that swine of a landlord – and swirled its contents. In the light from the mass of candles that filled the hall, he watched the lees gather in the centre, and continue moving in their orbit once the surface of the liquid was still again.

Grimald tore off a piece of mutton. "Eat up, Roderic," he urged with a menacing jollity. "The paupers we've let in would trade their teeth for food of this quality. You insult our King by not enjoying it." He bit off a lump of flesh that filled his mouth. Chewing that should keep him quiet for a while.

Rodi looked about the hall. Sat cross-legged either side of the ceremonial entrance, the paupers were tucking into their bread soaked in meat juices, washed down with beer. As often as told, they joined in the shouted acclamations in two languages praising the royal hospitality.

For the moment, everyone ate in moderate silence. Barking away in a dialect Rodi could barely follow, the minstrel was deep into celebrating the sack of Milan. It was gory stuff. Still veiled, the Queen Mother wasn't amused by the listing of atrocities. Every so often, she put up a hand to stop the Latin translation whispered into her ear – as if she'd really forgotten her own language. Of course, the Latins in the hall couldn't follow a word. Whether that was for the best, or was a lost opportunity for dissension between them and their Lombard masters, Rodi couldn't be bothered to say.

Beside his mother on the high table, the King *was* enjoying himself. He gurgled and chattered. He banged the table. He drank from a horn that spilled wine down his front with every swig. He seemed at one point to be pleasuring himself under cover of the table cloth. Sundarit, sat immediately left of the King, picked at a dish of olives, mostly drinking deep. His face was a thoughtful blank.

The feast was going as advertised. Everyone of note was in the hall. The grandest sat at the high table. The two other tables, long and lower and placed at right angles to where the grandees were showing themselves, were filled with the lesser folk. Rodi sat near the end of the left hand table. On his right, club out of sight, though not forgotten, sat Grimald. To his left was some legal officer. He spoke Latin with an affected accent, but mostly communicated in grunts and belches.

No Aripert, though. The place where he was most likely to sit, right of the Queen Mother, was ostentatiously empty. Rodi hadn't seen him at the seating of the grand people. He'd missed the King's speech of welcome, read out in slow Latin. He'd not been there for the opening courses, nor for any of the entertainments.

With a spluttering gulp, Grimald finished biting his meat into pieces that he could swallow without choking. "We always win, you know," he said, tipping his head at the minstrel. "When my grandfather came here, he took a harem of raped nuns." He dabbed at his mouth with a napkin. "I don't deny he's burning in Hell for it. But he and his sort drove the Greeks out of Italy like frightened pigs to market."

At last, the minstrel was finished. With a drunken roar, he dashed his harp to the ground and stamped on its strings. He staggered forward into the open rectangle of the tables. Ignoring the polite applause from the lower tables, he bowed to the King, and opened a ranting speech on the need to throttle the Greeks in Ravenna and to march against them in the South. The King's response was to climb onto the table and howl his approval. His face red as the livid sores about his mouth, the apparent depression of spirits he'd shown before the minstrel struck up was wholly gone. He bent down for a table knife and sliced with it at the air.

One of the rival Bishops fixed a smile on his face, and got up to bow at the King. The other, not to be outdone, threw a purse at the minstrel. The Papal Envoy got up from his place and crept round to whisper in the Queen Mother's ear. Her veiled head shook slightly – whether from laughter or agreement couldn't be seen.

The King overbalanced in the act of kicking some unseen enemy, and fell backwards off the table. He emerged a moment later from beneath the table, two gold bracelets held out for the minstrel.

Loud cheers now from all the tables. More purses thrown at the minstrel. The official next to Rodi made a long belching noise that reminded him of two camels he'd once seen in the Hippodrome.

Sundarit continued looking down at his olives. He didn't even acknowledge the praises heaped on him in the minstrel's improvised and unaccompanied second rendering.

But it was now over. From the corner of his eye, Rodi saw the thin eunuch get up and show his yellow flag to the paupers. They stood as one and went into one of the Lombard acclamations he'd taught them before the grand people showed themselves.

After this, another serving of beer. After that, a Latin poet. He droned his way through a set of verses so convoluted, even he must have had trouble making sense of them without a text in front of him.

After him, it was the fire eater. He should have been entertaining. Everyone else *loved* him – especially when he accidentally set fire to his own feet and hopped up and down while someone went off in search of a bucket.

Rodi took another sip of wine. In its own way, the long wait was as bad as if he'd been thrown into a dungeon after a racking. All that bore him up was the certainty that this was intended as moral torture. Before getting from his frigid bath, he'd given up on trying to question Grimald. No one else had spoken to him. Sooner or later, he would find out what Aripert had in mind for him. He might also learn if Scruto had turned him in, not to mention what would be happening to Scruto.

He thought of Scruto. Unless that swine of a landlord was lying, he'd been arrested too. He wasn't the sort who'd break down easily under torture, though he must have given something away of what he and Rodi were about. This didn't explain how anyone in Pavia could have known where to come looking, or that there was anything to look for.

He gave up on trying to think. If he wanted to know what Aripert wanted of him, he'd have to wait. Until then, sitting here as a sort of honoured guest was better than he'd have expected of barbarians.

On the whole, it was much better – though a water clock would have been welcome, to show the passing of time.

## V

Still in Jewish dress, Synesius limped into the open rectangle. "I Saul of Ephesus," he shrilled, "bring irrefutable proof of the existence of God, our Common Father."

He waited for the worried murmur to finish, and bowed to the King. He touched his forehead at the Bishops. He produced a rod of grey stone from his robe, and wheeled about, holding it above his head.

"By the authority of every philosopher, and by the common consent of all mankind, there can be no action at a distance. Whatever moves is moved by some other object, and must be touched by that object if it is to move." He turned again and moved closer to the King. "Will anyone here deny so self-evident a proposition?"

Someone made a farting noise. Someone else flicked a piece of bread at Synesius. It landed in his beard. He picked it out and let it drop to the floor.

"The only exception can be a miracle of God. Only God Almighty can set aside the laws of nature. And so, behold a standing Miracle of God, by which He reveals Himself to the world."

He opened his left hand, to show an iron nail. Holding this on his palm, he moved his stone rod closer, until, with a gentle click, the nail leaped upwards and joined itself to the stone.

A quiet groan went about the room. One of the Bishops got up and bowed to no one in particular.

"It's a trick!" someone shouted. "The old Jew's got a length of silk twine up his sleeve." Several people laughed. Another farting noise.

Synesius smiled. He looked round. He came to the far side of Rodi's table, stopping beside Grimald. "You are, Sir, a man of respectable standing in this company?"

Grimald nodded. He gave Rodi a suspicious look, before turning once more to Synesius.

"We have a volunteer of unquestionable veracity," the old man cried. He bent over Grimald. "Do take off the iron ring from your left forefinger. Take this rod in your hand – it won't harm you! Bring them together, until you can see for yourself."

"I think it would be better if I were to be your volunteer."

Unseen by Rodi, Aripert had come into the hall. Self-assured, a vision in green silk, he walked into the open rectangle. "Please step away from that table. There are young people sitting to it who might be alarmed by your mysteries."

He waited for Scruto to join him. Dressed also in green, he had a tired look about him – the tired, dreamy look that Rodi knew well. He didn't look at Rodi directly, but seemed happy to know he was there.

Aripert bowed to his mother and to the King. He turned to Rodi. "You are well, Roderic?"

"Yes, thank you, Sir." What else to say?

"Good. You are enjoying your dinner?"

"Very much, Sir. Thank you for honouring me with your invitation."

Scruto caught Rodi's eye. He looked away at once.

Aripert led Synesius away from the table. "What would you have me do, old man?"

"Your Highness, I require someone who has a piece of iron about his person."

Aripert laughed. "We Lombards have taken much gold and silver since we came into Italy, but are not yet unacquainted with iron." He waited for the polite laughter to die away, then took out a small dagger. "Will this be iron enough for you?"

Synesius glanced round the hall, His eyes fixed for a moment on Rodi. "Sorry," they seemed to say, "but this is one of those occupational hazards." He bowed to Aripert and passed him the stone rod.

Aripert held knife and rod in each hand. He brought them together. At about six inches, he frowned, moving the knife back and forth. At three inches, he let go of the knife, and watched it jump across and cling to the stone. His frown deepened. He held out his arm. He gently shook the rod. His knife moved a little, but didn't fall to the ground. Everyone began talking at once.

He held up his arms for silence. "There is no trick," he said to the gathering. To Synesius: "You have indeed shown irrefutable truth of the goodness and power of God the Creator of All. I can only wish now that you will carry your researches further, to the point where you confess the truth of His Son's Message and the errors of your own people."

Pious looks all round. The Papal Envoy pressed his hands together. The Bishops turned their faces heavenward.

He gave back the rod. "You have earned your dinner and more. Speak to the man who took your name and details. He will provide you with a purse of silver and a letter of thanks from His Majesty my brother."

He didn't wait for Synesius to shuffle out of sight, but moved straight for the high table, Scruto a few paces behind him. Men stood and bowed as he passed them. At the high table, he took his seat next to the Queen Mother. The man who'd been sitting to the right of his place, got up to make room for Scruto. They sat together. After a kiss on his mother's hand, he turned to whisper something in Scruto's ear. Scruto did now look at Rodi. He opened his mouth as if to shout across the forty feet that separated them. He changed his mind, and stared down at the finger bowl that one of the serving slaves put before him.

Aripert stood up again. "My dear friends," he began, "I trust you have enjoyed His Majesty's hospitality." It wasn't a question, or any invitation to comment. He paused for a momentary look about the hall. He continued: "My brother, the King, has an announcement to make. The custom of our people, and the importance of its content, would normally require this to be made in our own language. But half the guests of His Majesty do not know our language, and we are fluent in theirs. For this reason, he will make the announcement in Latin."

Not rising, the King gabbled his way through the text written on a half-sheet of papyrus. The nature of the Frankish threat required an immediate end to hostilities with the Empire. Sundarit was promoted to Grand Commander-in-Chief and "Dearest Friend of the King." Actual command in the field was given to half a dozen men whose names Rodi had never before heard.

Stumbling over the longer words, and with some whispered prompting from his brother, the King reached the last part of his reading: "I further declare that Aripert, my younger brother and *Very Dearest Friend*, has my full confidence in all matters. From this moment, none may approach me save through my brother."

He dropped his text and reached for his drinking horn. As one, two hundred pairs of eyes moved the few degrees from his face to Aripert's. The Papal Envoy then closed his eyes and began mouthing a silent prayer. The Queen Mother lifted her veil and sipped delicately at a glass beaker of wine. Aripert himself took no visible notice of the revolution he'd just worked. Explaining some basic rule of table manners to Scruto, he didn't even watch Sundarit rise from his place and leave the hall.

## VI

Much later, and in fresh clothes, Aripert sat back in a chair of gold and ebony. "I would allow you to sit on the floor, Rodi. But you will appreciate that my clothes might be spoiled, and I have no desire to see you naked."

Grimald pushed Rodi to the centre of a mosaic pattern on the floor. They were in a large room, though nothing on the scale of the banqueting hall. Its many lamps flickered and smoked in the breeze from the shuttered window. It was no longer raining, but the sudden cold brought by these latest showers now required a small charcoal brazier.

Aripert leaned forward, reaching for one of the documents arranged on a low table. "For obvious reasons, our conversation will be in Greek. Do not answer me in Latin unless it is plain that I wish you to."

He took up and unfolded and skimmed a sheet of parchment. He folded it again and tossed it across the room. It landed at Rodi's feet.

"Do you recognise the handwriting?"

In its own terms, it made sense that the Exarch had turned him in. What didn't make immediate sense was why he'd written to the Pope's Head of External Affairs, and why he'd insisted that Rodi was working entirely on orders from Constantinople.

Aripert broke in on his thoughts. "Scruto gave me a different story. I'll confess that his regard for you is unshakeable, and that this is the only reason I haven't decided to have the truth torn out of you with hooked gloves. But, while I have no doubt he is telling me the truth as he knows it, I'll be grateful if you don't repeat the cock and bull story you gave him.

"Tell me, Rodi – why is the Intelligence Bureau in Constantinople so keen to make trouble in Italy? Haven't you seen for yourself that everything is at peace? Our incursions into Imperial territory are mainly for show to our own people. There is no religious discord, and it is only a matter of finding the right miracle before we disestablish the Arian heresy and enter into full communion with our friends in Rome, and therefore in Constantinople. Hasn't the Empire troubles enough in the East and in the Balkans? Are we not worthy to share in the Empire's work of civilisation?"

Rodi could already count himself among the dead. He didn't need to keep himself from breaking down in tears, or from pleading, or from voiding his bowels into Aripert's fine clothes. He was calm and unafraid. He'd put on as good a show as Alaric in Constantinople could have wished.

He stepped forward to the low table. Aripert raised a hand to keep Grimald from trying to stop him. Rodi looked at the collection of documents. There, taken from their leather sleeve, and smoothed flat again, were the documents he'd hoped never to see again. They'd dogged him with ill luck since first sight of them in the Exarch's office. He was more interested in a letter he hadn't seen before. Closely written on parchment, it carried one of the Papal seals. This time, its meaning wasn't wrapped in an impenetrable cipher. But never mind its meaning – the script and general style were all he needed to make sense of what had happened. A shame the realisation had come so late. Too late, though, for regrets.

"You can take it for granted that I'm not a senior officer in the Emperor's service. I do what I'm told, and am given enough information to let me do it effectively. But we've known for some time what you were all up to here in Italy. You and your friends, the Exarch, and a clique of unknown size in Rome – all in it up to your necks with the pirates. Just because you have slaves to polish your fingernails doesn't mean you aren't a bandit spattered with the blood of the Empire's citizens."

Aripert smiled. "What our eunuch friend in Ravenna tells the Emperor will be sufficient to keep everyone who matters happy. But I see no reason not to be blunt with you, Roderic, born in, though not of, Aquileia. You can't rule people without taxing them. Tax-gathering is never by consent. One reason so many Italians put up with us is that, unlike the Empire, we don't strip them bare to fight insane wars halfway across the world. Even so, money still has to be raised. Fingernails don't polish themselves.

"I believe you have an interest in mathematics. Let us, then, construct a set of imaginary scales. On one pan we place the peace and relative contentment that Italy has known since before the two of us were born. On the other we place the suffering of those made victim to pirates whose activities the Empire is probably unable to stop.

"Will you say the balance of pains and pleasure is negative? I did nothing to set up the system of co-prosperity in which I am now a full partner. But I will do nothing to shake its foundations.

"And I will not allow you, Rodi, to go back to Constantinople with unhelpful tales of what you found in Italy."

Rodi walked back to Grimald. "And what of Scruto?"

"You did well to recruit him when you did. He only told me everything after I'd proved you had changed sides and already told me. But he's too good for you. Until I tire of him – which may be some while yet – he will do far better in my service."

He got up. He swept all the documents Rodi had found or produced into his right hand. "You are an accomplished forger, Rodi – though you'd have been more *authentic* in your efforts had you used a more complex cipher. It seems our diplomatic correspondence can be read by the Intelligence Bureau. No shame in that. But substitution ciphers really are for gross barbarians like the Franks."

He carried the documents over to the brazier. One after the other, he dropped them into it. The room was filled with the smell of burning parchment and papyrus. So much effort, now up in smoke.

After, he turned back to Rodi, triumph blazing from his face. "I've won, Rodi. I've saved Italy from war. I've at last stuffed that blundering old fool Sundarit. I've made myself a principal in a most profitable arrangement. I've laid hands on a divinely entertaining companion – and I'm not the man to leave *any* of his talents unused.

"And I've beaten you, Rodi. You were good. In other circumstances, I've have snapped you up as eagerly as I took Scruto."

He patted Rodi on the shoulder. "We shan't meet again. I can only hope that you enjoyed this evening's dinner." He switched into Latin. "You can take him now, Grimald. Do remember to make it painless."

## VII

The rain had left off. Hands tied behind him, Rodi was taken through a side gate from the Palace into a small street. From here into wider streets, emptied out by darkness and the weather. After a progress made slow by the need to avoid puddles, he was taken by Grimald under a long colonnade that led to an area of Pavia he didn't know.

They stopped outside a park enclosed by a wall and locked gates. Grimald put down his glazed lamp. "Stand where I can see you," he said. He took out a bunch of keys and fiddled with the lock. With a soft click, the oiled gate swung inward.

"Go though. Stand by the little statue. Don't brush against the wet brambles."

After the gate was relocked, they moved slowly towards the centre of what may once have been a communal garden for the rich. They came to an avenue lined with more statues. Long before, the path may have been gravelled or even paved. Generations of neglect had left it uneven, though still raised enough to be dry. At its end lay what had been an elaborate fountain topped by a statue of a laughing god.

Grimald put his lamp down, and went again through his keys. He bent and pulled open a bronze trap door. He stepped quickly back, a cloth held over his face. Even at ten paces, with the night breeze behind him, Rodi could smell the corrupted flesh.

Suppose he turned and ran? There was only Grimald. Though tied, he had faster legs.

Grimald seemed to read his thoughts. He pushed Rodi into a grotto set in the wall of the fountain. No escape. He leaned forward and cut him free. "Take your clothes off. Put them on that bench."

Rodi looked uncertainly at the lamp. He was beginning to shake from the inescapable horror of what was about to be done to him. His throat was closing over.

"I said *strip*. You can make this easy for me or hard for yourself."

Rodi closed his eyes. He took off the clothes he'd been given. He folded them and placed them neatly on the bench.

Grimald took his by the arm and pulled him towards the unlocked death pit. He pulled Rodi close to him, facing away. Rodi saw the glitter of the blade as it came closer.

Before the grip could slacken, he fell backwards with Grimald, landing on top of him.

He rolled free, and was aware of the cold wet of the fallen leaves on the ground. He tried to think. It probably wasn't a good idea to curl into a ball. It wasn't at all a good idea to start crying.

Synesius cleared his throat. "I told you, boy, there *was* a time!" With a groan and a creaking of elderly joints, he bent forward and lifted Rodi to his feet. He embraced him and kissed him on the forehead. "So little flesh on your bones. You should try eating more." He pushed the boy away and steadied him on his feet.

Grimald was only stunned by the blow Synesius had given with his walking stick. His eyes were flickering, and he tried to move his arms.

"Do bring me those fine clothes, Roderic. It won't do to have the evidence splashed all over me."

He waited for Rodi to fetch the heap of folded silk. With a deeper groan, he bent over Grimald. A quick move, and the throat was cut deep across. He pressed Aripert's clothes into the wound, damping the buzzing, gurgling sound, though not the convulsion of the legs.

He limped over to the bench and sat down. "We'll wait for the blood to stop gushing. Search me, though, how we'll carry the body ten foot for stuffing down that hole. The cold has buggered my poor hip."

Rodi sat beside him. This was the time for making a cynical comment about Aripert's clothes. Instead, he pressed himself against the old man and sobbed without control. Synesius took off his cloak and arranged it over Rodi's shoulders.

"My story will have to wait, Roderic. Yours too, interesting though it doubtless is. Some of my Jewish friends are waiting outside the park. They won't like to be asked for help with the body. But they will get us out of Pavia. All considered, I suppose we should give up on a trip to Rome. That means going back to Ravenna. The eunuch may not be displeased to see you. After all, you have done as he asked. Mind you, he'll not be dishing out any fatted calves."

Outside the grotto, there was a spattering of rain on the fallen leaves.

## Part Five – Ravenna, Sunday the 2nd October, 618 AD

# I

Eleutherius finished reading the last page of Rodi's report. He looked up, his face worryingly neutral.

"I don't think we'll be forwarding a copy of this to Constantinople."

"I thought you'd say that."

The Exarch counted the sheets. He pulled out the third and read again about the palace revolution Aripert had staged. "A fine combination of brevity and the telling phrase. Leaving aside your abilities in the field, Alaric must be proud of you. If I hadn't a better use for you, I'd appoint you Antony's replacement on the spot."

He got up from his desk and went across to the window. He waved at Rodi to stay in his place. "I will indulge you, Roderic, with the right to judge me. That being said, young Aripert made as good a case for our arrangement as can be made. I'll add that it was in place when I arrived here. All I've done is to make it more regular. Oh, there's little difference between a pirate and an emperor."

He leaned heavily against the window. The rain had left off again, and it was a fine autumnal afternoon. If Rodi turned his head, he'd see the spot where Antony had been butchered. That's what had started the wild ride of the lunatics terminating only when the gates of Ravenna swung shut, with him inside them.

But he didn't look round. Eleutherius was laughing. "Leaving old Synesius out of your report made holes in it you haven't done much to fill."

Rodi tried not to stiffen. "You know about him?"

"Twenty years before you were born, I endured one of his courses at the University of Constantinople. If he hadn't kept his head down so well, I'd have had him in here the day you arrived. We could have avoided so much unpleasantness. Such, however, is the sadness of life."

He came back to his desk and poured two more cups of wine. "Now to business. I need you back in Pavia. I can promise a more comfortable journey than your last round trip. You can have post horses and a flag of truce. The latter will be useful for those Lombards who believe we are actually at war."

Rodi managed not to spill his wine. "I don't think Aripert will be terribly pleased to see me again."

"Oh *pish*, Roderic! Aripert isn't a young man to bear grudges. Why, it's only a few years since I pulled up his tunic and spanked his bottom with both hands. He ran howling about his father's tent, before coming back to sit on my lap."

He smiled almost benevolently into his wine. "Of course, he won't be too pleased with the news you'll be carrying him. Nor will His Holiness in Rome. But we've managed to throw them into such a panic by letting them think the Empire's onto their part in the enrichment scheme, that none of them will have any choice but to recognise my accession.

"Same deal applies, by the way. You do me proud again, and I'll keep Father Cosmas not merely alive, but in greater comfort than he'd enjoy in that grotty monastery. I also undertake not to betray you this time. Better than that, I shan't have any need to drop you in it."

Rodi put his cup down. "What *accession* have you in mind?"

"Ah, but you won't yet have heard, Roderic." He stood up again. "Come over here with me."

Rodi followed him behind one of the filing racks. On a stand, still full of pins, he saw a purple robe big enough to serve as a tent.

"*What?*"

"Yes, Roderic – I've decided to declare myself Emperor. Heraclius is useless. Even Alaric can't win the Persian War for him. I think Italy deserves better than an absentee ruler, far off in Constantinople. All I have to do to unify Italy is adopt young Aripert as my successor. A blessing from the Pope, and I'll move the capital back to Rome. Everyone wins, don't you agree?"

Rodi leaned on the map table. He wondered if there'd been something in the wine served by Eleutherius.

"But – but you *can't* be an Emperor. You're a…."

Eleutherius ran a hand over the robe. "I shall, Roderic, be every inch an Emperor – well, *almost* every inch. And, once I've had it tied under my chin, I'll have the beard to prove it!"

Printed in Poland
by Amazon Fulfillment
Poland Sp. z o.o., Wrocław